The Island Files:
An Underground Field Guide to the Islands of Maine

Volume I: Visitors

by Joshua Anchors

Deer Run Press
Cushing, Maine

Library of Congress Card Number: 2020936510

...

ISBN: 978-1-937869-12-0

First Printing, 2020
Second Printing, 2020

Published by
Deer Run Press
8 Cushing Road
Cushing, ME 04563

In memory of Linwood Judd
and the lighthouse that he kept so brightly,
so dutifully, and so quietly

The names of some of the people, animals, and places in this book have been changed out of respect for the privacy and continued well-being of the various communities in the Gulf of Maine bioregion.

Table of Contents

What has made this nation great?
Not its heroes but its households.

—Sarah Orne Jewett

Introduction

I first learned about the existence of the Island Society on the morning of August 13, 2012, when Linwood Judd[1] introduced me to what remained of the Island Files in his charred tool shack on a small island in Frenchman Bay. This morning was the beginning of a remarkable five-year personal and academic journey that would lead me to visit hundreds of Maine's 4,617 islands,[2] allow me access to over two thousand pages of previously unread historical documents, and result in a fair amount of scholarly debate about the integrity of my doctoral dissertation.[3] This book, the first of three volumes,[4] is grounded in scholarly research yet intended for a general readership and, given the seemingly implausible nature of an organization such as the Island Society, is sure to stimulate further debate.

---

[1]Fourth generation lobsterman and fifth generation member of the Island Society. Deceased October 12, 2017, at Eastern Maine Medical Center (EMMC) in Bangor, Maine. No remaining family.

[2]To understand how the precise number of Maine islands was determined through a satellite mapping process in the early 1990s, see Philip Conkling's outstanding book, *Islands in Time: A Natural and Cultural History of the Islands of the Gulf of Maine.* Down East Books. 1999. (2nd Edition)

[3]Anchors, Joshua C. "Covert Social Networking in the Gulf of Maine: A Socio-Cultural Analysis of the Island Files, 1965-2009." (2017) The Graduate School. The University of Maine. Dissertation #2243.

[4]*Volume II: Conflict* is due to be published in April 2022, and *Volume III: Community* is due to be published in February 2024.

The persisting scholarly debate arises predominantly around the legitimacy of the the Island Files themselves and the veracity of the anecdotes they recount. Instead of getting entangled in these strictly academic debates—the *authorial originalism* argument versus the *interactionist socio-cultural* argument,[5] for instance—I have selected for this book twelve particularly notable submissions from the enormous amount of original source material and offer them directly to the reader in a lightly edited form.[6] The interpretive introductions at the beginning of each selection are intended to provide additional context on the individuals, communities, or places involved, as well as to situate each selection within the broader historical and socio-cultural framework of the Island Files. The supplemental information offered in the footnotes is based on a variety of sources, including eighty-two hours of archival research at the Maine State Library and the Boston Public Library, anec-

---

[5]The leading proponent of the authorial originalism theory is Dr. Stephen Ingraham from the University of Maine Anthropology Department. His essay, "A Pragmatic Deconstruction: Why the Island Files are Beautiful in Theory but a Fraud in Reality," was published in the *Annals of Anthropological Practice* (December 2017) and essentially argues that the Island Files were not written by a multitude of island voices but rather by one particularly resourceful and imaginative author. The leading proponent of the interactionist socio-cultural theory is Dr. Katrina Arfush from the Tufts University Sociology Department. Her essay, "Interrogating the Covert Network: An Alternative Research Framework for Questioning the Integrity of the Island Files," was published in *Anthropological Quarterly* (February 2018) and uses emerging social network theory to challenge the notion that the Island Society was a sophisticated and functional network of individuals acting toward a unified mission.

[6]Edits to original text are limited to corrections in spelling, punctuation, and syntax. No edits were made that change context, meaning, or narrative flow of original text.

dotal evidence based on personal observation or experience, and phone, email, or in-person interviews with sixteen different individuals.[7] As a final measure of scholarly corroboration, any readers wishing to view the authentic texts and see the corpus of weathered (and sometimes charred) Island Files with their own eyes may visit the University of Maine's Fogler Library Special Collections Archive, where all remaining documents are housed in their original form and accessible to the public by appointment.

In the three-year process of reading, cataloguing, and analyzing 1,624 separate submissions dating from 1965 to 2009, I identified three predominant themes, at least one of which could be identified in nearly every submission. The theme of this first volume, *Visitors*, features submissions that document the experiences of outsiders as they suffer, grow, love, fight, explore, and simply try to survive in Maine's island communities.

The islands have a powerful symbolic value. Some visitors see the islands as a refuge from the frenetic pace of mainland existence, a sanctuary where they can find peace, escape from their demons, forge new identities, raise children off the grid, create art undisturbed. For others, the islands represent either the rustic, hardworking values and charm of a bygone era, or a spectacularly austere and savage landscape that offers endless fodder for the canvas, the camera, the blank page. There are still others who end up on the islands with no pre-conceived notions, no underlying hope for how the islands may serve their needs or yearnings. Regardless of how one arrives, it is difficult not to romanticize the islands. They are detached, independent, hypnotic in their severe beauty. The great moat of the sea helps protect them from the outside

---

[7]All interviews, both in-person and via phone, have been transcribed and can be found in Archive #72009B at the University of Maine Fogler Library Special Collections.

world, yet also beats them relentlessly with its endless procession of waves and tides. One imagines that only the most resilient and autonomous souls can inhabit them. For most outsiders, they remain an enigma, an uncharted territory on the map, a fabled landscape where scavenger crustaceans reign supreme. The selections in this book simultaneously challenge and validate these notions, striving to reveal the rich complexity of an oft-romanticized landscape and the paradoxical truths of island existence.

Given the wealth of material pertaining to the central theme of *Visitors*, I have selected submissions for this volume that meet one of three criteria: 1) the material serves greater historical or biographical significance, such as the otherwise undocumented account of Jack Kerouac visiting Bailey Island after the Muhammad Ali—Sonny Liston fight in Lewiston in 1965; 2) the material serves to connect important dots—for family members, journalists, local historians, scholars, etc.— in a larger narrative, such as Jack Baptiste's disappearance from the waters around Andrews Island in the summer of 1996; and 3) the material, through my admittedly subjective lens, is simply entertaining, unusual, or has some degree of literary merit, such as Dean Sullivan's account of Patti Kittleburger and the emerald bikini.

Though this book highlights submissions that tell compelling stories, the vast majority of Island File submissions were brief and routine, offering succinct accounts of any occurrences over the course of the month that the author deemed notable. These submissions, which rarely included stories with a traditional narrative arc or developed characters in any significant way, touched on at least one of the following topics: community gossip, notable births and deaths, updates on large projects (e.g., construction of a schoolhouse, purchase of a new ferry), or reports of inter-island conflict or collaboration. Some of the submissions, however, deviate entirely from the format of a quasi-official report and seem to be written more as an informal letter to a friend or a relative. Of course, it is this eclectic collection of styles, topics, and voices that makes the Island Files so fascinating. It is also interesting to note the egalitarian nature of the Island Society in that all submissions, regardless of their content or their style or their motive, made it into the archive.

In order to provide an understanding of the range of topics and writing styles in these typical "business as usual" submissions that make up the bulk of the Island File archive, I am including three sample selections below, all originally handwritten and included here in unedited form.

Sample Selection #1

Matinicus Island, Penobscot Bay
Albie Winters
4 May 1984

Frank Myers retired this month after thirty-six years as Chief of Fire and Police. He's going to travel to Ireland with Judy and then join the town's budget committee when he gets back. It's a big change because Frank's been around for just about everything since I can remember.

Tammy Page's son Arthur left for the Army on Wednesday. We had a send-off party at the Ester's place that was fun. His basic training is at a fort in North Carolina. He says he won't be able to come back here until Christmastime.

The veterinarian from Augusta finally came out on the mail plane and was busy all day. He had to put away the Owens's dog and little Ellie cried for two days!

Somebody drew a Nazi symbol on the bulletin
board this month and Fred closed down the store a
few hours early. He told me that he thought only
one of the young guys could have drew it because
they didn't have to live through the war.

Thank you,
Albie

Sample Selection #2

Squirrel Island, Boothbay Harbor
Constance Moody[8]

3 December 1998

Dear MWIS,[9]

Another month gone buy and still no snow which is
fine with me. Heh. But I'm sure it will come sooner
or later. Corrine is coming today and we're going
shopping. Don't know what I need to buy (maybe
another extension cord!) but she worked every day
last week and didn't have a day off so today we're
going to make a day of it and then stop by to see
Bernard. Tomorrow Tony is picking me up for
Annette's wake at 10. I got my 5000 piece puzzle
all done and I won't take it apart until Lena comes

---

[8]One of Constance Moody's submissions, entitled "Final Jeopardy,"
appears in this volume.

[9]Master Wickie of the Island Society (MWIS). See page xiv for explanation.

home next month and can see how much she tortured me with that gift...heh! I think I'll paste it to a big peace of card board and put it in the garage so I won't have to put it together again if I get board. Got <u>all</u> my Christmas decorations up all by myself. One day when it comes time and I can't do it then I'll cut back and put a little Charlie Brown tree. Ha! Sad! Well, didn't leave the house much this month and was busy with this puzzle so I can't say much of anything that happened here except that Annette died and it didn't snow. Everything else seems about right.

Merry Christmas. God Bless.
Connie

Sample Selection #3

Chebeague Island, Casco Bay
J.R. Eklund
30 August 1966

-An engineer came out to look at the ferry slip and met with Jerry Jameson about some repairs
-The Whitington family from North Andover, Mass., bought Eddie Pederson's house
-Alex Todd pulled up a white lobster in his trap on the north side of the island on 11 August (see photo)
-One of Faye Woodcock's garages burned down and she lost a lot of rope and a few traps
-Bob Sherman passed away on 19 August from heart problems
-An Oriental man came out on the ferry on August 22 to do photography he said

-Nancy Upton won a blue ribbon for her banana bread at the Bangor State Fair
-Some big tuna catches early in the month and the boys on *My Other Life* were pretty happy

***

However entertaining, fascinating, or confounding the Island Files may be at times, it must be remembered that two great tragedies form the backdrop of their discovery and subsequent exposure to the public. First, the gradual decline of participation in the Island Society from 1972-1995, as is clearly evident in the waning volume of submissions over those years. This gradual decline is followed by a precipitous drop, from 1995-1998, in which average monthly participation decreases from fifty members at the beginning of 1995 to fourteen members by the end of 1998. Based on the historical pattern of submissions, it could be argued that as of early 1999 the Island Society, once an interconnected network of islanders organized around a unifying mission and with widespread membership across the Gulf of Maine, ceased to exist as a cohesive organization. After nearly three generations of activity ostensibly aimed at protecting island communities from outside influence, recording and preserving island culture, and resolving conflict based on a uniquely local and unwritten code of conduct, by the start of the 21st century the

Island Society had become a disparate assortment of isolated individuals, mostly older, longstanding members, who continued participating more out of a sense of routine and tradition than out of institutional purposefulness.

The second tragedy is the enormous loss of historical data resulting from an alleged act of vandalism in July 2012 that accidentally set fire to Linwood Judd's tool shack and, in the span of thirty minutes, incinerated seventy-one years' worth of Island Society submissions. At that time, Linwood served as the Island Society's Master Wickie, a name derived from archaic maritime parlance, referring to the lighthouse keepers who were sometimes called "wickies" because of their job trimming the wicks in the era when oil lamps and clockwork mechanisms were used. Not only did the Master Wickie serve the figurative role of keeping the light shining for the Island Society, but also performed the very practical role of receiving and logging all member submissions and storing the entire Island Files archive. The previous Master Wickie, Sid Hemmings,[10] who had served in this role for over twenty years, had unexpectedly passed away in the spring of 2005, and a decision was made to move the entire archive from a secure location on North Haven Island in Penobscot Bay to an island in Frenchman Bay owned solely by the Judd family. It remains unclear exactly how this decision was made since the Island Society leadership had largely disbanded in 2003 after several sudden deaths and an injury that required the most

---

[10]Originally from Isle au Haut, Sid lived most of his adult life on Hurricane and North Haven Islands. He was known as a leader within the Mid-Coast Maine region and an outspoken critic of various salmon farming projects in Penobscot Bay. He worked for twenty-three years as the Director of Facilities at the Outward Bound School on Hurricane Island and was thus well-known to many island visitors. He was awarded the Medal of Honor by President Reagan in 1991 for acts of valor during his service in World War II.

senior member, Dick Weber, to relocate to a hospital on the mainland. In retrospect, however, it is evident that the decision to relocate the entire archive was hasty and impulsive, resulting in an inadequate storage facility and, for Linwood, lack of clarity around the basic responsibilities of his new role. Though more than two-thirds of the archives was destroyed in the fire, including all files from the period when the Island Society was most active and omnipresent in the Gulf of Maine, it is a minor miracle from many perspectives—sociological, linguistic, historical, cultural, literary—that the most recent files survived. The silver lining of this latter tragedy, after all, is perhaps that it served as the impetus for the remaining files to see the light of day.

***

Despite all of the perplexing details that exist within and because of the Island Files, one of the things that still most mystifies me on a personal level is why Linwood (or perhaps others of whom I am unaware) granted me exclusive access to the Files and then gave me permission to reveal them to the public, first through my dissertation, and ultimately through this book and the two forthcoming volumes. This issue remains a mystery not for my lack of trying to learn Linwood's intentions or for lack of spending time with him; indeed, I have asked him directly several times, have recorded and transcribed a two-hour interview with him, and have spent many hours with him sorting through the remaining Island Files submissions. The direct questioning never got me far as Linwood often spoke in enigmas, with the guardedness of a Yankee and the inscrutability of a Zen monk. Moreover, the question of why he initially contacted me about this issue never seemed particularly pertinent to him. The only thing that mattered, in his view, was ensuring that the remaining Island Files were both preserved and released to the public in a dignified way.

In the wake of the fire, what remained in Linwood's tool shack were thirteen rectangular cardboard crates on wooden shelves, each labeled in black marker with a range of years (e.g., 1973-1977). The crates were filled with manila folders labeled in black block letters with location (e.g., Chebeague Island) and author (e.g., Barbs Kunkel). Each manila folder contained a combination of handwritten and typewritten pages, though mostly handwritten, with dates generally in European format at the top of each page (e.g., 17 March 1985) based on when the submission was mailed in. The other shelves in the shack were either empty and ash-covered, or contained the hollow skeletons of crates and the blackened, curled remains of papers and manila folders from the early years.

Several months into my research on the Island Files I came across a document in the 1977-1986 crate entitled *Brief Guidance for Island Society Submissions, 1916*. This was the first and only document that I came across during five years of research that seemed to have been issued directly from Island Society leadership to its active members. This is of significance for several reasons. First, it provides one of the few signs that the Island Society had some sort of central organization with an interest in aligning its otherwise fragmented membership along certain operating principles. Second, the existence of this documentation means that it is entirely possible that other such undiscovered "memorandums" were sent to members at some point throughout the life of the Island Society and lay in storage in a dusty island attic somewhere in the Gulf of Maine. My sincere hope is that any readers of this book with a connection—known or unknown—to the Island Society, will help create a fuller and richer picture of this organization by bringing such documents to light should they be discovered. Third, it is impressive that any grass-roots organization should exist for over three generations, and even more impressive that an organization should exist and thrive for so long with such little central governance or consistent messaging to its member base. This, I believe, is a testament to both the value of the core mission of the Island Society as well as its members' fierce pride and commitment to protecting, sustaining, and documenting the uniqueness of island life in the Gulf of Maine.

Given the distinctiveness of this document and the context it provides for this project, I have included below the original text in its entirety:

Brief Guidance for Island Society Submissions, 1916

One of the foremost tasks of a member of the Island Society is to maintain written documentation of particular occurrences in one's territory. Each member shall be the judge of what occurrences one feels is of value to document and submit each month. Many submissions will be brief and simply note the continuation of business as usual. Other submissions will be longer and will document in one's own voice anything perceived as out-of-the-ordinary or "of note." Such vigilance and keen awareness of one's environs is what allows our humble network to sustain itself and even thrive against many odds. We serve as the eyes and ears for a vast and rugged terrain. This requires a constant watchfulness, an attention to detail, and an observational acuity.

The intentions of the suggested guidelines below are to 1) efficiently facilitate the collection, organization, and response (on rare occasion) of a high volume of monthly submissions, and to 2) encourage members to personalize their submissions without being hindered by excessive concern for form and style.

1.   Write location, name, and date (month, day, year) on the top left-hand corner of the first page.
2.   Double-space submissions when appropriate quantities of paper are available; reserve single-spacing for times of limited paper supply.
3.   Place submissions in envelopes labeled MWIS and give to the appropriate local point of contact around the end of each month.
4.   There are no stylistic or narrative guidelines. Write using one's own voice.
5.   One should write as much or as little for the month as one feels necessary. There is no required word count.
6.   Include drawings, maps, charts, or other supporting documents/objects with submissions when appropriate.
7.   Do not include second-hand information in submissions. All submissions should be based on personal observation.
8.   Avoid editorializing or sharing personal opinions in sub-missions. The objective is to document occurrences in straight-forward language.
9.   Members must not be overly concerned about grammar, punctuation, syntax, spelling, paragraph transition, etc. What is important is members' commitment to duty and unity.

Yours In Fellowship,
The Island Society

This memorandum raises three critical questions that drive to the heart of the Island Society's existence and mission. First, why does the memorandum call for such a degree of "vigilance" and "constant watchfulness?" What are the perceived threats to island life? Why this unrelenting emphasis on islanders' unification? How will this unconventional approach of documenting "occurrences" and dispatching submissions to a central archive help protect and preserve island communities? Second, was the Island Society an intentionally secretive, underground organization, or was its "secrecy" merely a function of being located in a remote terrain and making no discernable mark on the outside world? If the organization was not deliberately secretive, how could someone like me grow up in a Maine island community for eighteen years and never know about the Island Society? Third, what was the desired outcome for the collection of Island Files? Was this archive created as a means of documenting history and culture in a unique and relatively isolated part of the world, or did this collection of submissions serve more immediate, concrete objectives of which we are now unaware?

Ultimately, what is the legacy that the Island Society intended to leave behind? That of an underground organization huddled in a defensive posture, bent on preserving itself against real or perceived external threats? Or is the legacy more benign? That of an organization simply trying to build relationships and community, holding together the people and ways of a disparate and undisciplined terrain, cultivating connection and unity through the essential, basic, and collective task of storytelling, and in the end leaving behind a rich and eccentric regional historical record for future generations?

I believe that the intended legacy was most likely a peculiarly complex combination of these two extremes and that we will never determine with absolute certainty the origins and the true motives of this organization. Though a cottage industry of critical approaches and theories on the Island Files seems to have blossomed within academia since the publication of my dissertation, this is not a book of academic discourse, but rather, as Linwood had hoped for, a book of exploration, of excavation, and of respect and honor for a multitude of island voices from across the generations. I leave the theory and deconstruction and academic discourse to other books. All I intend in these pages is to help readers discover and celebrate the curious and fantastic legacy of this singularly unique organization known as the Island Society.

The Island Files:
Visitors

Selections from 1965-2009

The edge of the sea is a strange and beautiful place.
—Rachel Carson

Selection #1—The Emerald Bikini[11]
Islesboro Island—Penobscot Bay
Denny "Dean" Sullivan
15 July 1997

The seclusion that makes island communities so unique and charming is also what makes them so challenging to inhabit and to visit. This selection captures, on an almost trivial yet somewhat heartbreaking scale, the most fundamental of these challenges: transportation in an environment where ferries often serve as the only "bridges" to the mainland. The ferry plays an essential yet subtle role in this selection, as it does in so many island narratives, and its presence, or non-presence, ultimately serves as the emotional turning point for this story.

This selection's setting is a rare exception within the Island Files in that most of the story takes place on the coastal mainland rather than in an island environment, though I would consider the story's defining moment to take place on an island. Another distinctive feature of this selection is that it is one of the rare personal stories, in the style of a heartfelt journal entry, that appears throughout the Island Files. While many submissions include authors' thoughts, opinions, and judgments, and often interpret events, or "occurrences," through subjective lenses, few other submissions are written in such emotionally raw and honest language. Reading this selection can feel like surreptitiously leafing through the emotionally-charged journal of a teenager in the throes of love and heartbreak, a sort of free-form Rimbaud bearing his sensitive, manly soul to unknown readers.

---

[11]Unless otherwise noted, the titles of all selections are mine.

Joshua Anchors

The author of this selection was raised on Vinalhaven Island and was 19-years-old at the time of this submission. Dean is now married with four children and lives in Biddeford, Maine, where he manages a physical therapy practice. When I spoke with him in March 2016 about this submission, his only one on record in the Island Files, he did vaguely recall the events recounted in his submission, though he had no recollection of either what he wrote or that he had submitted those pages. As for this story's protagonist, Dean says that he did not see her again after she departed on the bus to Wilmington, though he was able to confirm that her last name was Kittleburger. She is now a member of the Twelve Tribes Family in Ithaca, New York, and has changed her name to Emunah. She declined to speak with me on the phone.

***

Patti took a bus up to Rockland from Honesdale, Pennsylvania, and I met her at the bus station with Ben and Zack who couldn't believe—I could see it in their eyes—that a hot girl like her had come all the way up here to visit me. She was tan and wearing a tank top and jean shorts and had these crazy muscles from rock climbing and hiking and canoeing all summer in the Adirondacks. The first thing she does when she sees us is say, *ha, you guys all look so Maine,* and then hugs me in a great laughing embrace, jumping up and wrapping her legs around my waist so that I lose balance and almost fall down. We take her backpack and her guitar (she can only play one song, "Wish You Were Here," by Pink Floyd, but still carries the guitar everywhere) and we all get into my pickup truck, with her between me and Ben, and she half-sits on Ben's lap which makes me a bit anxious but luckily the drive is short. We go to Gritty's Tavern and get Patti a hamburger and we all get beers and I tell the story about her faking an orgasm on the sidewalk in Lake Placid, NY, in front of a bunch of bewildered Japanese tourists with cameras, and the story about her collecting discarded grocery store receipts so that she could get reimbursed by the summer camp for more than we had spent on the kids. She tells the story of the first day she met me and how that night I hooked up with another camp counselor named Mo in my platform tent in the woods. Somehow Mo was super sensitive to the touch and a really loud lovemaker and the whole crew could hear Mo trembling and moaning with pleasure all night and thought I was a super lover. Then Mo hooked up with another guy a few nights later and we heard the same thing so the myth of my lovemaking was crushed.

We ordered a second round of beers and Patti told us that she spent basically all her money on the bus ticket up here and needed to make some cash somehow. We all told her we'd give her twenty bucks or lend her some money, but she said she knew what it was like to be poor and work hard and never liked to borrow or take from friends (stealing from strangers was another matter), so we brainstormed ways she could make cash over the next few days on the Maine coast. We ultimately determined that there weren't many legal ways of earning cash in just a few days, especially since she didn't have a car or any fishing skills and only wanted to work half days so that she could spend time with me exploring. I got to feeling a little down during this conversation because Patti's father was in prison in Virginia and her mom was a pill addict in Florida and she had a step-brother she didn't know well and she had lived her life up till now floating around, earning a few bucks here and there, and it just felt suddenly sad to be trying to drum up a few hundred bucks in a few days so that she could move on to the next place where she'd have to drum up a few hundred more bucks, though part of me hoped that maybe she'd want to settle down with me in Maine for a while and take a break from the nomadic life.

Then Zack pumped his fist and said that she should do the Saturday night bikini contest at The Bounty in Bangor. He'd heard there was a $300 pot for the winner. Patti wasn't a voluptuous body kind of girl but she was rock-hard and sculpted and tan and athletic and had exotically-angled eyes and we thought it was a great idea and all agreed to leave for Bangor around 6PM from my house so that we could make it to the auditorium a bit early and scope it out. Zack said he knew one of the bouncers there and said that he may be able to get us in for free. Ben said he knew a few guys from the Bangor High School football team who may be able to round up some other guys to come vote for Patti. We strategized: it was all about audience votes so we needed to stack the audience. I was brainstorming how to get a bunch of guys from Rockland and Rockport and maybe even Vinalhaven to drive all the way to Bangor when Patti announced that she loved the plan but didn't have a bikini. We laughed and shrugged—that seemed a simple enough issue. We had four hours to find a bikini that fit Patti. And also heels. And maybe some earrings or a bracelet or something.

We decided to split up: Ben and Zack would work on spreading the news and hopefully getting a crowd of supporters to show up in Bangor and I would help Patti procure the outfit. Ben tossed out the idea of just driving up to Bangor Mall and buying a bikini, but the idea was soundly and swiftly rejected. That would have eaten up a big chunk of the total winnings, and if she didn't win then she was out $40 just for a stupid bikini. And anyways, she didn't have $40 to spend. I thought first of Annette, one of my ex-girlfriends, who was the same height and general build as Patti though softer. I was so caught up in the drama of the moment—of somehow finding a way for Patti to enter the bikini contest—that I started making calls without stopping to think what I was really asking for: to borrow a bikini from my ex-girlfriends or female acquaintances so that my current girlfriend (I think/thought), whom nobody had met and was from out-of-state, could enter a bikini contest in Bangor. Annette said she was working at the restaurant in Camden until 9pm and couldn't take off time to go home to go through her swimwear. And no, we couldn't go through her clothes drawers without her present. Willow, a former high school classmate of mine, was not particularly amused with the request and said she only had one-piece bathing suits. Amber, one of my friends since elementary school, invited us over and let Patti try on one black and one hot pink bathing suit but both were a bit slack in the waist and sagged in the butt. I was fine with a bit of sag—I was loving this whole adventure—but Amber was firm in saying that we couldn't let Patti go onstage with a saggy bikini. Amber said her best friend lived on Islesboro, was Patti's size, and had at least three bikinis because she'd gone swimming with her a few times last summer. Amber called Abby to organize everything and we took off for Lincolnville to take the ferry to Islesboro.[12] The timing would be super tight in that the last return ferry would get back to Lincolnville at 8:00pm and we'd have to drive fast to Bangor to make the contest by 9:00pm. Abby was there at the dock when the ferry pulled up and she and Patti acted like they were old friends and I realized that I knew Abby from indoor track meets at UMaine that we used to compete in during high school and where she was a star sprinter and I was a terrible long jumper. We reminisced a bit about those days and how Orono seemed like such an overwhelming metropolis at the time, and as she drove us the mile to her house I thought how perfect it was that Patti would be borrowing a bikini from an island girl who drove a stick shift pickup truck and didn't ask any questions about why we needed the bikini or who Patti was, etc.—to her it seemed the most natural thing in the world that we urgently needed to borrow a bikini late on a Saturday afternoon.

---

[12]The Margaret Chase Smith ferry is operated by the Maine State Ferry Service connecting Lincolnville Beach and the island of Islesboro. In July of 1997, the ferry made the three mile, twenty-minute passage approximately 8 times on weekdays and 12 times on weekend days or holidays.

I wait outside chatting about the Red Sox with Abby's younger brother on the porch and then Patti comes outside in an emerald green bikini with black heels and washboard abs and I'm in awe and Abby's poor brother gets a hard on and needs to turn away. I'm filled with a spontaneous joy and pride that this is my girl and pick her up in a great hug and am dying to make love to her right there but Abby comes out and says the ferry leaves in 15 minutes and we need to hurry up and drive back. Patti changes back into her clothes, Abby drops us off at the dock and wishes us luck, tells me I can give the bikini back to Amber. We wait at the dock with a few other folks and I'm playful and frisky and Patti only lets it go so far before she shakes her head and says that she isn't a pile of meat, she needs to get in the zone for the show. Neither of us has ever seen a bikini contest but we speculate and theorize on the format, what happens and what Patti will need to do to seduce the audience. I don't have a watch but I know that we've been talking and waiting for more than 15 minutes so I ask one of the guys waiting if he knows how long until the boat gets here. He said it could be a bit longer. Fridays last run they usually load it up with supplies in Lincolnville, so it's always late, he said. I look at Patti and notice that something grim has set in her face. She stares with hollow eyes and a blank expression out at the distant shore. I tell her that we'll make it, that we'll drive fast, that the contest will start late, but she just sits there in a trance, not seeming to hear me. The ferry comes about 45 minutes late and I stand up and reach for Patti's hand but she pulls away. During the drive to Bangor I replay the afternoon in slow motion to understand where I went wrong. Was I too lustful in front of Abby's brother? Was she upset that I took us all the way to an island for a stupid bikini? Was she jealous of Abby? The song "Building a Mystery" by Sarah McLachlan begins playing on the local radio station and I finally ask Patti if she's upset, if I did something wrong. She turns to me and smiles in the dark, puts her hand on my shoulder. "I think I'm fine," she says. "Sorry. I just wanted the ferry to come on time. I feel like those little details are always off in my life. And those little details add up. And they hurt after a while."

We arrive in The Bounty parking lot at 9:25 and Patti changes in the car as I rush in and see Ben and Zack and a few other people I know near the entrance and they run toward me and ask what happened and I scream that the fucking ferry was late and they understand and no more needs to be said about that and they tell me that the registration is over and that the bouncer is firm about "no more fucking registrations" and it's a $15 cover charge anyways which none of us wants to pay so we go back to the car and break the news to Patti who just smiles and asks what we're going to do now, and we decide to go buy a case of PBR and drink it at Richard Afuma's apartment in Old Town. Our three cars pull up to Richard's and we're glad he's home because we don't want to drive back up to Rockland tonight and we tell Richard that we're going to drink and crash at his place. He was an eccentric Cameroonian exchange student at my high school[13] who looks exactly like the famous San Francisco 49ers wide receiver Jerry Rice and is now a grad student at UMaine and is always up for a good time and has a mostly unbroken tent so that two people can stay outside. We drink and laugh and get rowdy in Richard's terribly untidy bachelor pad and he brings out his traditional drinking horn at one point and Ben plays a Rusted Root album really loud and Zack starts having a pushup contest against a kid from Hampden and at one point Patti takes off her shirt to reveal the bikini top that she's wearing beneath it and we cheer and chant for her to show the bikini bottom though all she does is take Richard's horn and make phallic dancing

---

[13]Richard was one of two international exchange students at the Vinalhaven School during the 1992–93 school year. He lived with the Surrey family and often visits them during the holidays.

gestures with it then makes eye contact with me as the song ends and seems to get embarrassed and sits back down. The guys are revved up now. Zack begins doing a mock strip tease of his own and Ben taunts one of the Bangor guys with lap dance gyrations.

I had moderated my drinking that evening because I assumed that Patti and I would sleep in the tent, but when the crowd eventually died down and the two guys from Bangor left she curled up on the filthy couch and Richard brought her a blanket. I sat next to the couch and thought about asking if she wanted to sleep in the tent but instead I just said good night. She touched my shoulder as I was getting up and asked me if I could drop her off at the Greyhound station in Bangor in the morning. Richard had told her that there was a 10:00am bus, and she still had $20 of her own, and Ben had given her $10 for some reason. All she needed was another $15 to get to Wilmington. I was furious, confused, anguished, but once again I just said sure and headed out to the tent where I chain smoked four cigarettes and gazed up at the stars and felt terribly hurt and cowardly and infinitesimally small and insignificant.

The next morning we arrived at the bus station twenty minutes early and I gave her $15. I asked why she was going to Wilmington. She said she had some friends, maybe an opportunity to make some money. I told her I was sorry the bikini contest didn't work out. She smiled, told me not to worry about that, she'd win it next time. I asked if that meant she'd be back up here. She leaned over and lightly kissed me on the lips and got out of the truck. She stood in line with a few other folks and I stayed in the truck to wave goodbye. When she got to the counter I saw her dig through her belongings and start to talk to the older two men standing nearby, then one of them handed her some bills and she got her ticket and blew me a kiss just before she boarded the bus. About ten miles away from the bus station I realized that she hadn't given the bikini back to me. Something about that emerald green bikini made me enormously sad and I chain smoked again as I drove back to Rockland and thought about how things might have gone differently if that ferry had arrived on time.

Selection #2—The Beekeeper
Long Island—Casco Bay
Natasha Pixley-Miller
22 September 1987

Many island communities attract artists who seek sanctuary from the distractions of the modern world and find inspiration in the raw natural beauty of the Gulf of Maine. Most of these artists, however, visit for several weeks or months during the summer, or spend extended vacations at their island getaways, but few have the courage or fortitude to commit fully to year-round island life. The author of this selection, Natasha Pixley-Miller, is one of these few.

Originally from Long Island, New York, Natasha moved to Long Island, Maine, in 1949, at the age of 23, and married island native Stuart Miller in 1952. In an interview with WERU Community Radio in 1992, aired four years before her death, she said that she chose to move to Long Island, Maine, in the same instinctual way that an eider knows it's time to fly south for the winter. "Moving to a great hunk of granite in the middle of the ocean," she said, "was just in my bones."

Prior to moving north, Natasha had been on a steady path to becoming a reasonably well-known poet in East Coast literary circles, having published poems in the Atlantic, Prairie Schooner, and New York Quarterly. She wrote very little in the two decades after her marriage to Stuart, though in 1977 she published her most celebrated poem, "Meditations on the Puffin," in the New Yorker, and then began submitting poems to regional literary journals over the next decade. She eventually gained a reputation as a distinguished New England poet and was posthumously awarded the Book Award for Poetry from the Maine Writers and Publishers Alliance (MWPA) in 2001.

This selection was submitted by Stuart three months after Natasha's death and is accompanied by a brief introductory note as well as Natasha's obituary from the Bangor Daily News. Stuart passed away in 1994 and is survived by three children, all of whom live in southern Maine. This is Stuart's only submission in the Island Files archive, and "The Beekeeper" is one of only four poems that appear in the archive.

The protagonist of this selection, Henri Tremblay, grew up in a poor French-Canadian family on Long Island and left home when he was sixteen. He became the apprentice to a successful nomadic beekeeper in St. Agatha, Maine, and ultimately took over the operation in 1971. According to Henri's ex-wife, Elaine Sturgeon, his illiteracy nearly led to the business's collapse during his first year of ownership, so she began managing all the paperwork while he focused on the manual labor. She left Henri in 1983, the business collapsed shortly thereafter, and Henri returned to Long Island in 1984 after 30 years away. He committed suicide in 1989.

***

Dear Island Society,

Please accept this poem from my late wife Natasha who fiercely loved these islands and their people. She was a special woman who saw beauty everywhere around her and had a magical, lyrical way of carrying herself through the world. I submit this unpublished poem as an homage to this woman whom I loved so dearly – the woman who wrote about these islands with such tenderness and beauty for so many years, and who would marvel at the idea of her writing being sent out to sea and into the hands of unknown readers.

Warm regards,
Stuart Miller

PS: Please find enclosed Natasha's obituary for your reference. Though she was not a member of the Island Society, I do hope that you see merit in retaining this poem for your collection.

*****

PORTLAND—Natasha Pixley-Miller passed away peacefully in Portland, Maine, on June 12, 1987 with family by her side. Natasha was born on April 17, 1926, in Islip, New York, to Aaron Pixley from Saugerties, New York, and Marsha (Peruzzi) Pixley from Scituate, Massachusetts. Natasha was an only child and in her youth was a gymnast, an *en point* ballerina, and a drill team leader. She was very close to her paternal grandparents Hazel Ardis Pixley and Prescott Pixley of Westhampton.

After graduating from Bay Shore Consolidated High School with High Honors in 1943, Natasha stayed with her aunt in Manhattan for three years where she took evening classes at the City University of New York (CUNY) and worked as an office clerk at the Box & Knightley Law Firm. During her years in

New York City, Natasha became friends with several reputable women poets and eventually began studying and writing poetry herself. In September 1948, the *New York Quarterly* published Natasha's poem "Queen Anne's Lace," and shortly thereafter Natasha left her job and committed herself full-time to poetry. In the ensuing four years, Natasha earned a reputation in East Coast literary circles for her spare, perceptive, and poignant verse that focused on the more subtle intersections between nature and humanity.

In the summer of 1952, Natasha traveled to Brunswick, Maine, to visit the family of one of her literary friends, Abigail Turner, and stayed in a small guest house overlooking Maquoit Bay. Several weeks into her visit she attended a local gathering and met Stuart Miller, a fisherman, local newspaper columnist, and resident of Long Island. Natasha moved to Portland at the end of the summer in order to continue her courtship with Stuart and to concentrate on writing poetry about the Maine Coast. Her poem "Maquoit Bay," a five-part ode to the small, picturesque bay that served as her introduction to coastal Maine, was published in the *Paris Review* in February 1953 and garnered widespread praise in the poetry community.

Natasha married Stuart in the summer of 1953 and moved to Long Island (Maine), a place she rarely left in the ensuing three decades. There she raised three children, served on a variety of local committees, and for five years taught English, French, and geography at Long Island Elementary. Natasha turned her attention back to poetry in 1976, after her children had all moved to the mainland, and published her most well-known poem, "Meditations on the Puffin," in the *New Yorker* in 1977. Over the next decade she published sixty-three poems in over two dozen regional publications. Her poetry served as an unmitigated celebration of the Maine Coast and all of its human and non-human inhabitants.

Natasha is survived by her husband, Stuart Miller, and three children, Robert Miller, Rachel Miller-Levine, and Nicole Miller. Services will be held at the McGowan Funeral Home, 470 Deering Avenue, on June 16, from 1:00 p.m. to 8:00 p.m.

Natasha had a life-long love for the natural beauty of coastal Maine. In lieu of flowers, her family requests that donations be made in Natasha's name to the Maine Coast Heritage Trust in Topsham.

***

Joshua Anchors

The Beekeeper

Regardez le ciel. Demandez-vous: Le mouton oui ou
non a-t-il mangé la fleur?
Et vous verrez comme tout change...

—*Le Petit Prince*, Antoine de Saint-Exupery

I.

He stood with an electric saw outside the honey
      chamber
grimacing
pressing down
on the fresh corpse
with bees everywhere
and rivulets of viscous bear blood
vibrating
and swimming up
the quivering steel teeth.

II.

Midwinter in southern Florida
twenty or thirty miles west of North Palm Beach
and the bees rebel.
Under midnight moon
they swarm.

Heat
balm
clover
orange blossom
great purple-headed thistle
and a thousand or so males
clinging to cloth and mesh
pulling bellies against him
piercing the white cloth
and with final lunge-thrusts
pushing in
and dying.

III.

In the beam of headlights
a beekeeper
silhouette
moving quickly
through
black bears
black flies
black forest
clouds of
goldenrod
raspberry
wildflower
nectar.
A flat on forklift

and he curses
tabarnak
câlice
crisse
six wounds
to the wheel

but this is
his work:
hands swelling
crushed bees against skull
a firecracker for the bear
a bee in the collar;
pounding
rusty rebar
with rubber
hammer far past
midnight
way up north
in a field
in the high beams,
onstage.

IV.

Full hives
pregnant
with throbs
of lovely

delectable
gold
on the way
home
in the old flatbed
with only eight miles
per gallon
and gears all gone
and a few hundred thousand
honeybees
humming
along I-95.

V.

Home.
A log cabin
in Madawaska
down a dirt road
that winds up
a hill and field
of wildflowers
and a thousand
broken frames
jumbled together
broken by
black bear
some spring evening
when the

beekeeper and his wife
went into town
for pizza
for a change.

VI.

Change.
In a distant land
a goat ate a flower
and all changed
irreversibly and
incomprehensibly
for the beekeeper:
a note
beneath a glass
honey jar
instead of a wife
on the porch
and he can't understand
the note or life
because the note's
in English
and life
is too hard
and someone must
take care of
the flowers
the bees

the punctured tires
the engines
the firewood
the swelling hands
the hives
the home
the beekeeper
all the work to be done.

VII.

He takes the ferry
and comes back home
to us
to his mother
to the house
of his past.

He sits with her
on the porch swing
in the ochre dusk
looking out at the gulf –
the vast breathtaking
interminable gulf –
thinking and
drinking and
brooding,
feeling hollow
and useless

and numb,
like a comb
without honey,
a hive
without bees.

VIII.

Somehow:
this far from shore
there is a single bear
on the island,
a loner
a contrarian
a glutton,
and it feasts
on honey
and beeflesh
this spring.
The bear awakes
the beekeeper
and the game begins.

IX.

Virginal flowers
laden with pollen
bend heavily
in undulating grasses

in the meadow
where the beekeeper
sets his trap
of hives.

But time has passed
and things have changed
and the game is no longer
with bear
but with self,
and while he waits
in the tamaracks
by the edge of the meadow
brooding drinking thinking
a bee stings
the softening beekeeper
and, for the first time,

he winces
in pain.

Selection #3—The Mercer Family
Great Cranberry Island—Blue Hill Bay
Edith Gilbert
26 March 1981

An ongoing challenge for many Maine island communities over the past fifty years has been preventing the younger generation from moving to the mainland while attracting younger, child-bearing families to move out to the islands. Without an infusion of young blood and new families, island populations can quickly dwindle, becoming populated exclusively by an elderly demographic and, in the most extreme cases, go extinct from one generation to the next. As childbirth becomes increasingly rare on Maine islands and the younger generations are drawn to the economic opportunities on the mainland, some islands are forced to think creatively about how to maintain their populations and attract young families. One strategy that some communities adopted to attract these families, who were occasionally referred to as "breeders," was to use grant money from various organizations to offer prospective families year-round accommodations, plots of land, and building supplies for free or at an extremely discounted rate.[14]

This submission centers around one family, the Mercers, who moved to Great Cranberry Island in 1976 as part of the island's attempt to attract a younger generation and create a more dynamic community. Since this was before the introduc-

---

[14] The following two sources provide detailed information about the housing grant program used by a coalition of island communities: "Maine islands using grants to attract new residents" from *The Boston Globe* and "No Island is an Island: Maine's Island Housing Groups Collaborate" from *Communities and Banking.*

tion of formal housing grant programs for island communities in 1998, the residents of Great Cranberry voted in 1975 to use municipal funds to offer discounted real estate to five young families over the course of ten years. Although this program experienced significant setbacks due to funding challenges and the Mercer family tragedy,[15] its thinking was ahead of the curve and the Great Cranberry Housing Settlement Program became the basis for future projects that would receive state funding[16].

Written in the style of a photo-documentary, this submission traces the author's intimate relationship with the Mercers during their tragically short-lived time on the island. The original submission, as it was received by the Island Society, was twenty pages of handwritten material with the relevant photo taped above the corresponding text. Edith Gilbert, the author of this submission, was 32-years-old in 1976 and was the second youngest full-time resident on Great Cranberry at that time. Her daughter, Alexandra, was the only child under five-years-old on the island and, were it not for the addition of the Mercers' young boy, would have been the only child in her grade at the island school. "I fought hard for new life on this island, not only for my sake but also for Alex," Edith told me. "I wanted her to grow up with playmates and classmates."

---

[15] The Mercers were the first family selected for the settlement program and moved onto the island in the summer of 1976. Their log cabin burned down on the night of December 17, 1980, and all three members of the family were tragically lost in the fire. The incident was widely reported by news outlets across the state and led to the introduction of several fire safety regulations. A touching profile of the Mercers can be found in an Ellsworth American article entitled, "A Family that Brought Hope to the Cranberries." (January 6, 1981)

[16]The following article provides a historical overview of the Great Cranberry Housing Settlement Program: "Trying to Get One Step Ahead: A Brief History of the Great Cranberry Housing Settlement Experiment." Darcy Waverly. Journal of Maine Life and Times. Fall 2006.

Edith comes from a family of fishermen that has lived on Great and Little Cranberry Islands for three generations, and she claims that at least one member of each generation was actively involved in writing submissions for the Island Society. She wrote her first submission in 1968 after finishing college in Rhode Island and, in a rare move for a college-educated woman, decided to permanently relocate back to Great Cranberry instead of accepting a job offer in New York City. "I have always treated my submissions like journal entries," she said. "There's something cathartic about writing out my feelings and sending the pages off into the unknown. Sometimes I journal my joy, like when I first moved back to the island in '68 and fully understood my love for this place. Other times, like in this case, I journal my sorrow and grief."

***

It's taken me months to write this because I didn't want to sit down with these photos and look at those three beautiful faces again. Only four years here and they made quite an impression on this place. Grace with her exotic Southern accent that eventually charmed us all. Bill with his quiet and gentle intensity that helped earn the fishermen's respect. And little Atticus with his head of blond curls and his fabulous name that nobody'd ever heard before. I remember back when we made the decision to begin the settlement project and how afraid we were that we'd get troubled families who were just looking for dirt cheap land. Instead we get the perfect family, and now that they're gone everybody's absolutely torn up. Since the fire, I think some people here have even lost hope. That's what the Mercers came to represent to a lot of us – a light of hope for the future of this island. Now a lot of folks just feel empty, like something very valuable was stolen from us and we'll never get it back.

*

I took this photo of Grace during our first long walk together. She'd lived here for a few months by that point but I think every waking minute of her and Bill's time was spent clearing land and building that house. We walked all the way out to Deadman Point and the whole time we chattered like old friends. I remember she wanted to sit on the cliffs for a few minutes and watch the seagulls swarming behind Eddie Hull's boat. It fascinated her, everything about the ocean and the fishermen and the seagulls and the way the crabs scuttled through the seaweed at low tide. All those things that I took for granted back then, before I started spending time with Grace.

*

This is a photo of Bill on the Great Cranberry wharf looking down at a bucketful of fresh-picked mussels. He was allergic to shellfish and I always found it funny that he ended up living on an island of lobstermen. In all the photos I took of the Mercers, Bill always looks like this—thoughtful, quiet, and serious. His face was always turned slightly downward like he was studying something on the ground. I first thought Bill carried around some great life sadness, but the more I got to know him the more I came to believe that he was actually one of the happiest men on the island. He adored Grace, he enjoyed the hard work of clearing land and building the house, and he loved Atticus with a patience and gentleness that I'd never seen before between father and son. Atticus stuck by Bill's side during the entire summer that he was building the house and Bill would calmly explain every step in the process and answer all of Atticus' questions as if he were talking to a man and not a child. I remember visiting their place one summer afternoon when it was nearly finished and Atticus asked Bill why they had to put a roof on the house. What struck me was that Bill took the question very seriously. He told Atticus to lay down next to him on the house's fresh pine floorboards and look up at the sky. He asked Atticus to imagine what would happen if he was sleeping in bed and it began raining or snowing without a roof on the house. Atticus silently imagined the scenario for a moment, then began giggling and repeatedly squealing "I'd get wet" as Bill reached over and tickled his armpits and they began mock-wrestling in the fresh sawdust. Grace and I sat on two stumps in the yard sipping sweet tea and watching Atticus rub handfuls of sawdust into Bill's long beard, and I knew then that I loved these people because they were different, and because they were tender.

*

In the days after the fire, the most heartbreaking moment for me was telling my daughter Alex what had happened. She and Atticus had become inseparable and their friendship was one of the reasons I spent so much time with the Mercers. Alex was staying at her father's place in Ellsworth the night it happened and I didn't have the heart to tell her over the phone. When she returned home several days later, I remember bringing her onto my lap, stroking her hair, and trying not to cry as I told her that Atticus and his parents had left and were never coming back. I'll never forget her reaction, the way she looked up at me with a defiant expression I'd never seen from her before and told me that Atticus was her husband and couldn't leave.

That was their game from day one: make-believe marriage. Alex first saw Atticus at the controlled brush fire on Rice Point on a Saturday morning in May 1976, and she went right up to him and said that her name was Alex and that they were going to play the wedding game. Atticus gave a solemn nod and they walked off to the edge of the field to make preparations. The only two three-year-olds on the whole island—it took them a few months to find each other but once they did they rarely left each other's side.

I took this photo after one of their rare squabbles on a day when Alex threw a tantrum because Atticus said that he didn't want to play the wedding game. He said he wanted to play the log cutting game instead. Grace intervened beautifully, speaking softly to both of them, holding their hands, and asking them to pose together for a photo. They pouted through the photo, Atticus standing, Alex crouching, both looking grouchy, and seconds after the shutter clicked they were off chasing a groundhog at the edge of the clearing. Then half an hour later Atticus was back to making Alex a wedding crown of daisies and dandelions. And for the hundredth or so time in three years, they acted out a quick and serious marriage ceremony and then went off into the woods to play.

*

Grace and I took a lot of long walks together during the weeks when Bill's brother Frank was visiting from Texas to help with the house. We'd leave Atticus and Alex behind with the men and we'd usually walk out to the cliffs at Bunker Head or Deadman Point. We'd pack a bag lunch and sometimes I'd bring my camera or my water color kit and Grace would bring her recorder or her journal and we'd just sit on the cliffs for hours. The gulls always kept a close watch on us during these outings, mostly because they hoped for bread crumbs and leftovers from our lunches, though I also like to imagine it was because Grace enchanted them with her simple recorder music. This is the photo I took on the day when Sturgis Franklin was hauling traps right nearby and apparently had a good day. He saw Grace at the baked bean supper a few nights later and joked that her music-making on the seashore a few days back had brought him good luck with the lobsters. All the men around the table laughed and said that Sturgis needed all the good luck he could get. This is the night I think that Grace and Bill really began to feel at home here, when they just became part of the jokes and were folded into the laughter without effort. A few fishermen started referring to Grace as the Siren, a good-humored nickname more to poke fun at Sturgis than anything else.

A few months ago at the wake Sturgis got up to say a few words and read a poem called the Siren Song by Margaret Atwood. The librarian had helped him find it earlier that week and it really tore everyone up.

*

I took this photo at the beginning: before the Mercers' first winter on the island, before their cabin was built, before Atticus and Alex were friends, before I began taking long walks with Grace. It may seem odd, but this is one of the most difficult of the Mercer photos for me to look at because I know what eventually filled this empty space. I know the hard work and joy and love that took place on those three acres of land where they built their cabin. I ended up spending so much time in this space. Now, without them, the space seems hollow and gloomy, almost dead to me, as if none of that joy and discovery ever occurred. Someday I'll get over that feeling, but not quite yet.

I see Atticus over by the dirt pile on the left hand side, walking amongst the logs and the soil and the earthworms, shirtless as always, loose diaper hanging low. How I would have loved to have seen him become a young man in this space.

*

Bill had a stubborn vein and insisted on doing every step of the cabin himself. From the bark stripping to the foundation laying to the roofing, he wanted to do it with his own hands. He said he'd prefer to do things slowly and thoughtfully rather than pay a bunch of guys to throw up a house in a few weeks. Aside from Grace, the only person who helped him with the hard labor was his brother Frank who came out to the island for three weeks in August and kept pretty much to himself. Unlike some men, Bill's stubbornness wasn't ornery or authoritarian. He just knew what he wanted and quietly and politely persisted in doing things his way, even when he was sometimes mocked for being backwards or old-fashioned.

I don't think Grace would have minded one bit if the cabin were thrown up in a few weeks by paid labor, though she appreciated Bill's vision and perseverance and never pressured him to take shortcuts or stray from his vision, even if it meant living in a platform tent for nearly four months. Though I remember how happy she was to move out of that stinky tent!

*

This photo got me looking back through all my photos from the past few years and made me realize that I don't have a single photo of the Mercers' finished cabin. This one here is the most advanced stage of the building process that I captured. It was early August, Bill's brother Frank had arrived several days earlier, and they were making good progress putting up the walls. I don't remember why I took this particular photo on that particular day, but looking at it more closely now I see a certain quality to this image that I probably hadn't intended at the time. There are several frames: Atticus plays with his sticks and sawdust in one frame, Bill and Frank take a break and eat lunch in the second frame, the skeleton of the cabin is being fleshed out in the third frame, and in the fourth frame we see the cabin in context, surrounded by the woods and fields and wildflowers of this beautiful, lonely island. As always, Bill has a slight downward gaze. Atticus is nearby but not dependent. There is a stillness, a patience. The type of contentment that comes with hard work and clear mind.

*

This photo is from the picnic we had on a Sunday afternoon in early September out on Fish Point. It was one of the only times that all six of us were together—me, Grace, Bill, Steve,[17] Atticus, and Alex. The Mercers and the Pommeroys.

---

[17] Edith's second husband, Steve Pommeroy.

It's also one of the only photos of me with the Mercers, despite all the time I spent with them. Steve had taken Atticus and Alex down to the tidal pools and on his way back he snapped this photo with my camera. Now that I'm really looking at this photo for the first time since the fire I think it's kind of amusing that we all look so glum and serious when in reality we spent the whole afternoon laughing and having fun. Though I do remember that Grace told me it just about killed Bill to have to stop working that morning because the cabin was almost finished and all he wanted was to finish the job.

*

I took this photo from backstage when Bill, Grace, and I went to see someone[18] speak in Southwest Harbor. It was our

---

[18] The speaker was Scott Nearing (1883-1983), a radical economist, educator, writer, political activist, and advocate of simple living. He was a popular figure in the homesteading movement for his commitment to integrating simple living with a life of social justice. A prolific writer and scholar, he became particularly influential through his books *The Making of a Radical, Man's Search for the Good Life,* and *Living the Good Life* (co-written with his wife, Helen). According to Marty Howells of the Southwest Harbor Historical Society, who attended the talk on December 14, 1980, Scott Nearing spoke about the simple pleasures of homesteading and the virtues of self-sufficiency, vegetarianism, and pacifism.

first time off the island together without Atticus and Alex. I forget who the speaker was, but I know that Grace and Bill had read one of his books and thought he was a worth listening to. We got to the talk early and Grace started talking with the speaker's wife and before you know it they invited us to sit onstage because of the settlement project. The man said that he wanted to use us as examples for his talk since we were living the type of lives that he would be talking about. Leave it to Grace to make friends with a stranger and get us all invited onstage! I was so embarrassed up there because I'd worn my ripped up pants and now I had to be sitting in front of all these people. I did get to take this photo, though, and I love how the man's wife is knitting off to the side as if she couldn't care less.

This was three days before the fire.

*

This is the last photo that I took of any of the Mercers. Atticus striding down the Vernon road with his boots and blue sweater and a smile on his face with those great deep dimples. Bill had been teasing Atticus during the walk by singing Arlo Guthrie's pickle song[19] in a funny voice.

I don't want a pickle

Just want to ride on my motorcycle

And I don't want a tickle

'Cause I'd rather ride on my motorcycle

And I don't want to die

Just want to ride on my motor....cy...cle

Each time Bill got to the last line he would sing real slow and really ham up the final "motorcycle." I'd never seen Bill so goofy. I'd never seen the family so happy. And me too, I was happy. This was contentment. Though I would wake up the next day to a nightmare, this photo reminds me of the contentment I felt that morning with these very special people, this very special family. For that I am blessed. For that this whole island was blessed.

---

[19] Edith is referring to "The Motorcycle Song" by Arlo Guthrie.

Selection #4—Dear Sandy
Beals Island—Western Bay
Sanford "Sandy" Cockburn
1979-1983

A strong regional identity is often defined as much by the quirks and eccentricities of the people of that region as it is by the region's natural environment, local traditions, and unique linguistic features. The institutions that allow these regional eccentricities to shine usually come in a variety of forms and mediums, including public-access TV stations, local newspapers, historical societies, or centralized gathering places such as barber shops, diners, or post offices. For over two decades, one of the most cherished forums giving voice to the inhabitants of coastal Maine was an advice column in the Machias Valley Times named "Dear Sandy." Modeled on "Dear Abby," the nationally syndicated column, "Dear Sandy" focused on offering advice and commentary, oftentimes with a humorous twist, regarding questions, concerns, and ethical dilemmas that were strictly local in nature.

The author of this column, Sanford "Sandy" Cockburn, was known as an eccentric local character in his community of Beals Island and is rumored never to have stepped foot off the island throughout his lifetime. A sickly child, Sandy regularly missed long periods of school and was unable to engage in most physical activities. While his peers fished and played baseball, Sandy spent his childhood reading books and taking leisurely strolls around the island. Lacking physical stamina and a formal education, Sandy was confined to working a variety of odd jobs on Beals Island, such as tax preparer, part-time librarian, school photographer, and curator at the small maritime history museum.

In 1963, U.S. Senator Edmund Muskie visited Beals Island on a brief campaign stop, and Sandy, at the age of 27, was asked to give him a tour of the island's notable sights. Clearly impressed, Senator Muskie praised Sandy before leaving the island, calling him "wise beyond his years," and this one tour, which lasted less than an hour altogether, established a local reputation for Sandy as an erudite and sage-like presence in the community. Several months after the Muskie visit, the Machias Valley Times approached the Sandy with the idea of writing a weekly column on local history and culture. This column gradually evolved into the popular "Dear Sandy."

Though the "Dear Sandy," column existed from 1965 through 1986, Sandy submitted the column to the Island Society only during the years of 1979-1982. These columns, thirty-one in all, are his only submissions in the Island Files, and it is unknown why he submitted only during this short timeframe. This selection includes seven letters from this column that not only reveal Sandy's distinct style but also highlight the practical community function that his column served. Unfortunately, the Machias Valley Times closed its doors in 1992, and their historical archives were lost in the flood of 1994,[20] so the only centralized collection of the "Dear Sandy" column is found in the Island Files archives.

A bachelor his entire life, Sandy Cockburn passed away in his sleep on Beals Island in 1999 and is buried in the Sewell Field Cemetery. He has no living relatives. The epitaph on his tombstone reads, "Well, that was interesting."

***

---

[20]"A Spring Ice Jam Bursts, and a Maine Town is Pummeled." The New York Times. April 19, 1994.

Dear Sandy,

Last month my wife and I ate at that Chinese restaurant on Church Street [Beals Island]. It was packed and the food was pretty good. We tried to go there yesterday but learned that it had gone out of business. What's the story?

Yours truly,
Hungry for Noodles, Jonesport
November 1980

***

Dear Hungry for Noodles,

Indeed, Sunrise Kitchen was known for having the best chicken chow mein this side of Ellsworth and it's a shame to see them gone. A true loss for all Chinese food lovers in the Downeast!

Believe it or not, the Machias Valley Times refused to fly me over to China to conduct first-hand research for this response, but as usual my network of global informants helped me get to the heart of your question. Here's what I learned:

Sunrise Kitchen opened at its 29 High Street location in 1970 as Wong & Zhang's #1 Famous Blue Ribbon Gold Star Chinese Restaurant. The two cousins who co-owned the restaurant, Ding Wong and Yulong Zhang, were originally from Shenzhen, China, and had worked at several restaurants in Boston's Chinatown prior to moving north. It remains unclear how they learned about Beals Island and why they decided to open a restaurant there, but the fact remains that they were pioneers in what has now become a very modest but stable Chinese restaurant industry in coastal Maine. Both men spoke rudimentary English, lived in a loft above the restaurant for the entirety of their nine years on Beals, and were rarely seen outside the restaurant.

According to Mr. Henry Colpitts, the owner of 29 High Street, the restaurant struggled mightily in its first three years and had few customers. Despite this lack of business, he said that the men never missed a rent payment and were otherwise very respectable tenants. The restaurant underwent a makeover of sorts in 1975, changing its name to Gold Star Rising Restaurant, creating a more "traditional Oriental" ambiance, and offering Italian, Thai, Japanese, and Vietnamese dishes on the menu alongside its standard Chinese fare. Business began picking up in early 1976 when the restaurant first offered its $0.99 all-you-can-eat noodle buffet on weeknights.

In 1977, a short-lived controversy broke out involving the restaurant when Jim Hamill wrote a letter to the *Machias Valley Times* accusing the restaurant of promoting Communism, referring to the symbolic rising gold star in its name. Virtually overnight the restaurant changed its name to Sunrise Kitchen and offered a special $1.19 American Patriot Buffet. Business was steady, by all accounts, from 1977–1980, and at some point during those years Yulong Zhang's wife moved over from China to help in the kitchen.

The only insight into why Wong and Zhang closed the business so abruptly in the fall of 1980 was offered by Jane Alexander who assisted the men with tax preparation during their time on Beals. She said that the men always spoke fondly about their hometown and said that they wished to return there someday when the economic conditions improved. Apparently last month the men received the green light to return[21] and decided to pack up camp in our dear little part of the world, leaving behind a lot of hungry noodle eaters and, from what I hear, three large boxes full of #1 Famous Blue Ribbon Gold Star fortune cookies.

Sandy

***

Dear Sandy,

A couple from New York City bought a big house up here about five years back and since I live next door they pay me a little bit just to keep an eye on the place. As far as I know they haven't come up to the place since they bought it and I haven't had to bother them at all. Anyway, this spring I'm having my house renovated and won't be able to stay there for a few weeks so I was wondering if you think it would be all right for me to stay in their place while the work is being done on my home? I don't want to bother them if I don't have to. What do you think I should do?

Thank you for your advice,
Caretaker with a Conscience, Mid-Coast Maine
May 1979

***

---

[21]Mr. Wong and Mr. Zhang's hometown of Shenzhen was indeed an economic beneficiary of what is now commonly referred to as the Open Door Policy. Under this policy, which was announced by Deng Xiaoping in December 1978, Special Economic Zones (SEZ) were set up in certain regions of southern China to attract foreign investment. According to Dr. Hualun Zhou, the Chair of Fordham University's Asian Studies Program, "Shenzhen was the first SEZ to be established and it showed the most rapid growth, averaging a very high growth rate of 40% per annum between 1981 and 1993, compared to the average GDP growth of 9.8% for the country as a whole."

Dear Caretaker with a Conscience,

That's quite a conscience you've got. Why are you asking me? Ask them! Otherwise: No, no, no.

Sandy

***

Dear Sandy,

I'm hoping you can help me with a debate I've been having for the past few months with my brother-in-law Dale. We're big fans of WWF[22] and we both went to the show at the Cumberland County Civic Center a few months back. That's where we saw André the Giant and Tito Santana beat the Wild Samoans in the Main Event. After the match Dale went to the Porthole to get a drink and swears that he saw André the Giant walk down the dock and get onto the 10:30 ferry to Peaks Island. I keep telling Dale that he must have had a few drinks too many that night, but he swears to what he saw and asks how he could mistake André the Giant for anyone else. He's got a point. Could you investigate?

Sincerely,
Giant Mystery, Hancock
December 1980

***

---

[22]The World Wrestling Federation (WWF) changed its name to World Wrestling Entertainment (WWE) in 2002.

Dear Giant Mystery,

What do you think I am, a private investigator?

Well, I must admit that your story did pique my curiosity so I decided to deploy the elite Special Investigations Unit at the Machias Valley Times to see what they could dig up. After months of tedious research, they managed to bring back three intriguing facts but no definitive conclusion on the issue. Fact #1: The match you saw at the Cumberland Civic Center was on August 30. According to WWF fight logs, André the Giant fought against the Ultimate Warrior in El Paso, Texas, the following night, August 31. Fact #2: Dr. Henry Simpson, the world's foremost expert in acromegaly (the hormone disorder from which André the Giant suffered), retired to Peaks Island in 1976 after a long career at Massachusetts General Hospital. He and his wife both passed away in 1979. Fact #3: The only hotel on Peaks Island, the Diamond Cove Inn, does not have the name André in its guest list for the night of August 30. Nor does the Bluebell House, the only bed and breakfast on the island. The 10:30 ferry was the final ferry of the night, so anyone taking that ferry would have had to stay on the island until the 6:00 ferry to Portland on August 31.

Make of these facts what you will. The real puzzle to me is why anybody would be interested in watching a WWF match!

Sandy

***

Dear Sandy,

You'll never believe it but I was cutting up a big cod for dinner last night and found this Army man (see photo please) inside its belly. I was going to throw it away but my husband Rich

47

said that these things can be worth lots if their [sic] collector items. Do you know if this is worth something?

Thank you!
Cod-tcha by Surprise, Hupper Island
July 1982

***

Dear Cod-tcha by Surprise,

Congratulations! What you've got there is a vintage 1973 G.I. Joe figure known as the Captain Cobra Commando (CCC) and he's worth a whopping $11,500. So what are you going to do now, go to Disney World!? Just kidding. I have no idea what he's worth and I don't have the slightest idea how to find out. Maybe bring him to some toy store in Camden the next time you head to the mainland. The question I have for you is how big was that darn cod?

Sandy

***

Dear Sandy,

What's the story with Keep Your Eyes on Your Fries Café out by Bass Harbor [Mount Desert Island]? Why did it change its name from Jimmy's Diner last year? I almost never go there because the muffins are too expensive, but I'm still curious.

Yours truly,
Eating My Fries, Gouldsboro
September 1981

***

Dear Eating My Fries,

First, glad to hear that you aren't overspending on muffins. I think I read somewhere that the #1 cause of bankruptcy in America is overpriced muffins, so kudos to you for keeping your hard-earned money in your pocket.

I recently called up Jimmy Hogan, the diner's owner, and here's what he told me happened there on November 17, 1980: a middle-aged man from out of town had breakfast (hopefully not a muffin) at the diner and put a $20 bill on the table upon finishing. Almost immediately after putting down the money a young man rushed up to the counter, grabbed the $20, put it in his pocket, and walked back to his booth. The visitor was surprised and decided to confront the young man. It quickly became a scene, with the visitor yelling and threatening and the young man cowering in the booth and a few waitresses crowding around. That's when Jimmy came out and calmed everyone down. He told the visitor that the young man, who had basically set up camp at one of the booths for the past three years, had some sort of obsessive-compulsive disorder that drove him to grab money whenever he saw it. "It takes a village to raise a mental retard,[23] "Jimmy told me, "and I'm just doing my part." He said that regulars to the café knew to hand over their money directly to one of the waitresses or else the young man would run over and snatch it. Jimmy talked the young man into returning the $20 and had a chocolate milk delivered to his booth. He also offered the visitor his breakfast for free. It was a good ending for all (except Jimmy who bankrolled a breakfast and a chocolate milk), and before the visitor left he kindly suggested that Jimmy put up a sign so that future outsiders would be aware of the situation and not cause a fuss.

As it turns out, a few months after this incident Jimmy was listening to the radio while making waffles and heard the following MacDonald's ad for the Big Mac.[24]

---

[23]The term "mental retard" was widely used to refer to individuals with intellectual disabilities up until the mid-1990s and was not considered disparaging as it is now.

[24]This ad was from the 1980-1982 MacDonald's Big Mac marketing campaign known as "Have you had your break today?" The version that Jimmy heard on Beals Island was actually the Canadian version and sounded like this in its entirety: *Have you had your break today? Easy does it on your way. So much to love, so little to pay, McDonald's is your break today, Have you had your break today? Fun on the run and it's coming your way. Save a little money, put a smile in your tummy, have you had your break today? Feed me, please me, tempt me, tease me. I'm havin' a Big Mac Attack. Two all beef patties, special sauce, lettuce, cheese, rush me down to Mickey D's. Have you had your break today? Keep your eyes on the fries don't let 'em get away. Nothin', nothin', like an Egg McMuffin, have you had your break today? Have you had your break today?*

I'm havin' a Big Mac Attack. Two all beef patties, special sauce, lettuce, cheese, rush me down to Mickey D's. Have you had your break today? Keep your eyes on the fries don't let 'em get away. Nothin', nothin', like an Egg McMuffin, have you had your break today? Have you had your break today? Jimmy liked the line "keep your eyes on the fries" and thought this would be a catchy new name for the diner while also hinting at the fact that customers needed to keep their eyes on their money. "Nobody from the outside will get it," Jimmy said, "but everyone on the island knows exactly what it's about."

I was tempted to head over to the diner for breakfast after speaking with Jimmy but, alas, the *Machias Valley Times* helicopter was being repaired, and the private jet was being used to research a story on Matinicus Island, so I had to take a rain check. Instead, I strolled down the street to LeBrie's Diner to get myself an average-priced and very tasty blueberry muffin. And I left my .50 cents right on the counter, thank you very much.

Sandy

***

Dear Sandy,

I had an idea the other day that I think would help the economy out here and wanted to make the pitch to you and your readers. What do you think about changing the time zone <u>one hour ahead</u> just for Moose Island? This would allow us do business with Europe and the rest of the world ONE FULL HOUR before the rest of the East Coast. We're already the easternmost island in the entire U.S.A., so this wouldn't be that much of a stretch. I think we'd see a lot of companies relocate out to Moose since they'd want to be one step ahead of their competitors. Manhattan was once just an island and now

51

it's one of the great cities in the world—the same could one day be said of Moose! Do you know how I can go about trying to change the time zone?

One Step Ahead, Eastport
December 1981

***

Dear One Step Ahead,

You're way, way, way over my head with this one. It's either totally brilliant or totally ridiculous. I'm far too cowardly to judge.

Readers—please weigh in by sending your coherent and respectful thoughts on this issue to the High Committee on Time Zone Opinions at the *Machias Valley Times.* And for those of you on Moose Island, enjoy the peace and quiet while you can!

Sandy

***

Dear Sandy,

I am in six grade and my science homework for next week is to write a one page paper about barnicles. Do you know anything about barnicles, like how they eat or if they can swim or how they make babies? I want this to be a good paper because my grade is really low in science and my dad told me maybe you can help (not write the paper for me but just give me information). I can't go to the library this week because I'm sick.

Thank you very much,
Barnicle Boy, Machiasport
1981

***

Dear Barnicle Boy,

I question your father's wisdom for recommending that you contact me regarding matters of Science. But clearly this is a desperate case!

First things first: spelling! B-A-R-N-**A**-C-L-E. Don't mess that one up or your grade's in trouble.

Now let's get down to business. How do they eat, you ask? Fork and knife? Straws? Chopsticks? I have no idea. But I'm sure they like cheeseburgers and fries. Who doesn't? Just don't tell your teacher you heard that from me.

Can they swim, you ask? Have you or your father ever seen a barnacle do a breaststroke? Or a forward stroke? Or any stroke for that matter? Well there you go.

How do they make babies, you ask? This is a family publication, Barnacle Boy—I have a reputation to maintain! Write a letter to Dr. Ruth[25] if you want a lesson in the birds and the bees (and the barnacles ha!).

---

[25]Sandy is referring to Ruth Westheimer (born 1928), better known as Dr. Ruth, who was a well-known American sex therapist, Holocaust survivor, and public figure who wrote over forty books about sex and sexuality.

So now you know why I make the big bucks, Barnacle Boy. This kind of scientific insight is based on a lifetime of observation and experimentation and field work. I just hope your teacher appreciates it. At least you'll be able to spell barnacle correctly!

Sandy

Selection #5 — "Lonely Pure Impossible-to-Believe America"

Bailey Island — Casco Bay
Wilson "Bunny" Mann
29 July 1965

The biographical literature about the Franco-American writer Jack Kerouac is so prolific and exhaustive that it seems difficult to imagine that a single evening of his post—On The Road life could be unaccounted for. Yet this selection captures one such evening in which Kerouac's whereabouts were previously undocumented by his myriad biographers. Perhaps of even greater significance than the details of Kerouac's wanderings, this selection offers a brief yet quintessentially Kerouacesque addition to his body of writings by including a formerly undisclosed handwritten page from one of his 1965 notebooks.

This selection highlights the remarkable capacity and omnipresence of the Island Society network in its active years. During these years, Island Society members did indeed serve as the eyes and ears of a vast terrain, always observing, documenting, and keeping a watchful eye on the island landscape. In this case, Jack Kerouac, the muse of the Beat Generation, pays a chance visit to a backyard boxing match on Bailey Island and is caught in the Island Society's great observational net. While the resulting submission does not add anything of particular significance to Kerouac's biography, it does provide for Beat Generation scholars and aficionados one more distinctive and unexpected piece to the remarkably peripatetic puzzle of Kerouac's life.

The submissions of Bunny Mann are copious within the Island files[26] and every submission begins in the same plain language: "The main thing worth writing about this month is…" Most months, the main thing worth writing about, from Bunny's perspective, concerned either the weather, the fishing industry, or updates on colorful or controversial local characters. He did write two other brief submissions about boxing matches, though neither provide the detailed descriptions that are found in this selection.

According to Dave Sackett, longtime Director of the Harpswell Historical Society, Bunny was ironically given his nickname due to his fierce temper, which was usually directed most vociferously toward the itinerant sternmen on his lobster boat who would refer to him as "bunny" behind his back. Bunny passed away in 1982 and his wife Marge passed away in 1990. Biggie Lawless and George Thurlow, the fighters described in this selection, are both now retired from jobs in the trucking industry. Biggie lives in Pittsfield, Maine, and George lives in Portsmouth, New Hampshire.

***

The main thing worth writing about this month is the night the famous author Mr. Kerouac came to the boxing match behind Andy Mancine's bait shop. Nobody knew he was coming, and none of us knew who he was for the first bit of time until Sid Hersey spread word that we had a special guest. Turns out he is one of the most famous writers in America!

Anyhow, it was a good night to come down because George Thurlow (we call him "Turbo") and Biggie Lawless were in the ring and both were undefeated on the local circuit. Andy wanted them fighting the same night as the Ali versus Liston fight

---

[26]Bunny Mann is the author of 57 submissions in the Island Files archives.

in Lewiston[27] and said he'd put money on either one of our boys against them pro fighters. I'd only seen George fight before and I couldn't imagine anyone tougher, but I've never seen a pro match before so I can't say.

Anyhow, the fight was supposed to start at 8:30 but Biggie didn't show up till after 10:00 because his car broke down and he had to hitch a ride from a tourist, then walk a bit. We had a few bottles and it was a good warm night so we didn't mind the wait, though I guess you could say we were pretty lively by the time Biggie arrived. Andy got the boys together to explain the rules and we all crowded up behind the ropes and listened while Pat Meeks took bets. About fifty guys were there to watch, mostly locals, but a few guys came down from Brunswick and a good crowd came over from Cousins Island to root for George. Andy rang the bell just after 10:30 and George took off like a snap and charged Biggie with some mean punches that didn't land, and then Biggie hit George hard in the chest and the fight was on.

Mr. Kerouac pulled up at the end of the first round with two other fellows. Sid told me that they were late because they'd driven straight here from seeing Ali fight in Lewiston.[28] And Ali won in less than two minutes. With a mystery punch,

---

[27] "The Night the Ali-Liston Fight Came to Lewiston." by *New York Times* writer Harvey Araton reflects on the significance of the 1965 Ali-Liston fight.

[28] Jack Kerouac's account of the Ali-Liston fight, entitled "What Was the Punch That Knocked Out Liston?," was published in the St. Petersburg *Independent* on July 10, 1965. The short article concludes, "You can bet your life: boxing matches are sad, and everything is sad anyhow, till that day when the Lion lies down with the Lamb."

they say. Imagine that! So I suppose that's why two of the fellows were in suits, because they were reporters, but Mr. Kerouac because he's so famous I guess was just wearing a white t-shirt and had messed up hair and didn't look anything special.

As I said, nobody knew who these gentlemen were when they arrived and Andy got real upset when they walked over. He tells us to keep quiet about these fights so the law doesn't get on his case.[29] Anyhow, he was about to charge over to them when Sid went over and shook hands with one of the suited fellows. He brought them over to where me and Andy was standing and we all shook hands real quick and then got back to the fight.

At the start of the third round Sid told me that Mr. Kerouac had written a bunch of books and especially the kids like him these days. As Sid told it, after the Ali fight all the sports writers went to a bar where some journalist for the Lewiston Tribune started telling stories about the fights he'd been to at Andy's and said that two of the big local guys were fighting this very evening. I guess everyone liked the idea of going to an outdoor fight on an island without all the flashing cameras and fancy outfits, so they drove right out here from the bar, an hour-and-a-half straight from Lewiston.
Biggie was winning pretty good into the seventh round and almost knocked George down a few times with his quick right hook. He has huge hands like his father[30] and every time George punched he'd just swat it away, then throw in a jab or hook to George's right side. Mr. Kerouac seemed to enjoy the fight and was right in there with the Cousins Island gang drinking straight from a bottle of rum and cheering for George even though he was losing pretty bad by then. I also saw that

---

[29]Andy Mancine was likely worried about Section 515, Chapter 21, in the Maine Criminal Code, which forbids "unlawful prize fighting." This section was revised in 1975, though a similar law was in effect in 1965.

all three of the fellows from away, including Mr. Kerouac, sometimes stopped to take notes on these small little pads. Andy caught wind of the notetaking at some point and went over to have a few words with Sid. It was one thing to let a few of Sid's friends watch a fight, but no way did he want any journalists writing about what happened behind his bait shop—fighting, gambling, drinking—all without a license.

Biggie won right at the beginning of the tenth round with a hook that seemed to just barely nick George's chin, but it must have connected pretty good because George went down hard and cold. Henry Tatum called the fight and another fight almost broke out when a guy from Cousins Island shoved Bill McIntyre, but Andy was able to break it up and everyone went back to drinking and talking about the fight. Sid told me later that Andy had told him to go over to the three writers and tell them that he'd appreciate it if they didn't write about the fight. They were all real nice about it and closed their notebooks. Sid said that Mr. Kerouac tore a page out of his notebook and gave it to him before he put away his notebook. Sid's been a member for a long time, of course, but he never writes reports, so he gave me Mr. Kerouac's page and told me that I may want to submit it in my report this month. I figured that a touch of writing from one of the most famous writers in America may be interesting, so here you go.[31]

---

[30]Biggie Lawless's father, Gary Lawless, worked in the granite quarries along the coast for over twenty years and is remembered by his peers for various acts of physical strength. Legend has it that Mr. Lawless once lifted a jagged 450-pound granite boulder over his head and threw it into the ocean off Peaks Island.

[31]Bunny included Mr. Kerouac's original handwritten page along with his submission.

the big one is covered in mud and the skinny one is covered in blood and both grunt snort punch and grapple sans mot so that the island children don't wake up and can continue their salty-air dreams rocked and cradled by the gentle waves beating relentlessly on the jagged rocky shore, and that's all that matters is the sweet dreams of the children

the devil lives in the immense unknown dark seaweed riddles of the ocean and Jesus in the ominous bloody skinny boy who looks like a sad haloed saint when he finally stands still & stops punching

this night this place these boys fighting by the forlorn sea is lonely pure impossible-to-believe america!

in the shadows a smoking wrinkled Buddha-man, and also probably fisher-man or lobster-man, given where I am, man, watches the fight with no excitement in his eyes but only a banana sliver of moonbeam on his weathered cheek

The big one is covered in mud and the skiny one is covered in blood and both grunt snort punch and grapple sans mot so that the island children don't wake up and can continue their salty-air dreams rocked and cradled by the gentle waves beating relentlessly on the jagged rocky shore, and that's all that matters is the sweet dreams of the children.

The devil lives in the immense unknown dark seaweed riddles of the ocean and Jesus in the ominous bloody skinny boy who looks like a sad holoed saint when he finally stands still & stops punching.

This night this place these boys fighting by the forlorn sea is lonely pure impossible-to-believe America.

In the shadows a smoking, wrinkled Buddha-man, and also probably fisher-man or lobster-man given where

I am, man-watches the fight with no excitement in his eyes but only a banana silver of moonbeam on his weathered cheek.

Selection #6—The South African
Swans Island & Mount Desert Island—Penobscot Bay
Marsh Burns
25 February 1998

The influx of tourists to Maine's coast during the summer months drives a great need for low-skilled, low-wage seasonal labor. Many of the workers who fill this need are college students from abroad who come on 90-day J-1 student worker visas[32] and are looking to earn American dollars and enjoy themselves in a beautiful landscape. The atmosphere at many resorts and certain high-volume tourist towns, like Old Orchard Beach or Bar Harbor, thus often feels like an international youth hostel scene, with carefree college students from around the world partying hard in their off-hours. This submission offers an unsettling glimpse into this scene of youthful summer laborers, and how this world, at times, may collide with local culture in particularly jarring ways.

The author of this submission, Marsh Burns, is originally from Swans Island and owned a high-end French restaurant, Bistro Champlain, in Bar Harbor from 1982-2006. A graduate of the New England Culinary Institute, Marsh also completed an MFA in Creative Writing at Bard College. Both restaurateur and creative writer, Marsh wrote one self-published novel under a

---

[32]The *Portland Press Herald* article, "By the numbers: J-1 student worker visas," provides data on occupations and locations of J-1 visa holders for the summer of 2017. According to a Department of Homeland Security spokesperson, Maine had far fewer J-1 visa workers in 2017 than in 1998 due to changes in immigration policy during the Trump Administration.

pseudonym,[33] as well as many short stories, essays, and poems, most of which focus on island life. He submitted many of his writings to the Island Society,[34] and in fact he has one submission in each of the forthcoming volumes of the Island Files.

In my email exchanges with Marsh, he wrote that this submission began as a novel but that he lost steam after this first chapter and ultimately moved on to other projects. The inspiration for this piece was a J-1 worker from South Africa who worked on the wait staff for one summer at Marsh's restaurant. "The guy was an awful womanizer," wrote Marsh. "He was really shameless. I saw a few of his antics with my own eyes and I think I kind of fantasize in this story about bringing him to justice, vigilante-style."

Marsh passed away from heart failure in January 2018, several months after my email exchange with him. Bistro Champlain is no longer in business and the space has been renovated into Geddy's Bar & Grill.

---

[33]Jaguar in America, published under the pseudonym Joshua Moyo (2008).

[34]Marsh made 58 submissions to the Island Society from 1978-1999. He was the most prolific Island Society member in terms of number of pages submitted, though Evelyn "Evie" Reed (see Submission #7 – Kyriacos) beats him out for total number of submissions at 117.

***

Chapter One—Island Justice

The day came, on Swans, when I needed to beat someone. A hot day, and humid, and I was fucking pissed. So I took the boat over to Tremont and drove to the Cadillac Pub with a stick of rebar. A long stick of rusty rebar. I was fucking pissed. I'd spent the day chain-smoking. Doing pullups on the rafters. Pounding a makeshift punching bag with Eddie. Thinking of Anna.

I left the rebar in the car and went inside, sat in a corner booth. A baseball game hummed on the television. Red Sox versus Blue Jays. The Red Sox were up 3-1. I couldn't give a shit. I ordered a rum and coke. Scanned the room. Took out a cigarette but realized I couldn't smoke inside. I slid the cigarette back in the pack, my fingers trembling.

Then I saw the back of his head. That thick-ass rugby-playing bull-neck. And the spiked hair. The black ribbed t-shirt tucked into tight jeans. Bright white tennis shoes, like some Eurotrash retard. Just like a few of Anna's friends had described him. The man who'd been hitting on her all night. The man who'd told her friends that he'd make sure she got back to her room at the Asticou without any problems. The man who'd bought her a drink just as her friends were leaving the bar. That was the fucker. Sitting on a barstool, a fresh girl by his side.

Anna had told me nothing. When I'd asked, during that heartbreakingly brief phone call a few days earlier, she'd told me to drop it, to let it go. Her summer in Maine was finished. She was at her parents' now, in New York, getting the help she needed. There was nothing I could do. So I'd made the trip over to the Asticou Inn and asked her friends. Who the fuck was that guy? The first girl had left early; she didn't know a thing. The second had told me that I shouldn't get involved. It was over. What did I want to prove, anyway? So I lost it. Right there in the huge sloping lawn by the tennis courts, I started screaming at her, this freckle-faced Dutch girl who'd left Anna all alone, in a bar, after midnight, in the hands of some asshole. What the fuck was she thinking? She was friends with Anna. And she was a regular at the Cadillac. She knew that scene. There's no way she couldn't have known.

The next two friends gave me details. His name was Simon, he was from Cape Town, and he was working the summer as sous-chef at the Jordan Pond House. He always sat at the bar, making conversation, buying rounds, telling a lot of stories about his rugby-playing days. That was all I learned. I'd had to pull the fucking words out of their mouths. Especially the fourth little shit. A dumb hick from Virginia who felt guilty as hell. Thought that he may literally go to hell. So why had he left Anna in that bar? Huh? What the fuck had he been thinking? But he didn't even have to tell me. I'd known immediately, as soon as I'd heard the news. I just wanted to scream at somebody who would cower. And he did. He cried and told me how sorry he was. He told me how one of the other girls had said that they should let Anna stay and get what she deserved. It would teach her a lesson about drinking too much like always and getting out of control. Robin had said that. The girl who worshipped Anna. Just like the Virginia boy worshipped Anna. They all did. They loved her for what they weren't. And then they punished her.

***

The girl sitting next to Simon wasn't bad. Not as pretty as Anna, but slender body, nice ass. She looked like a club girl. Probably from central Maine, Skowhegan or somewhere like that. Bangs standing tall with hairspray, tight white jeans, strapless black top, layer upon layer of makeup. Simon seemed into her. He kept ordering more beer and shots and leaning in close to whisper in her ear. Occasionally he'd point up at the baseball game and the girl would nod. He went to the bathroom once and the girl looked down at the table and rubbed her temples, yawned. Simon came back and ordered two shots, two more beers. The girl drank. Simon drank.

Then the baseball game ended. The Red Sox won and the mood in the bar became mildly celebratory. People ordered more rounds and began talking loudly and the bartender turned up the music. I ordered another rum and coke and sat there in my corner, still and watchful. Simon got up and walked to the far end of the bar. He waved to the bartender, pointed back to where the girl sat. The bartender nodded, laughed, put two beers on the counter. The girl adjusted her strapless top and looked up at the television. Highlights from the baseball game. Simon took a swig of his beer and walked back to the girl. He brushed his fingers lightly down her back as he came up behind her and she looked up at him and smiled, eyes half closed with drunkenness or tiredness or both. Simon gave her a beer and took a small pill container out of his pocket, dropped a pill into the girl's open hand. Probably told her it was an Advil or something. Like he'd told Anna. A date rape drug disguised as painkiller. Fucking asshole.

I followed them out of the bar fifteen minutes later. Simon clutched the girl by the waist, held her arm over his shoulder. He led her into the parking lot, her heels barely touching the ground as he pulled her like a sack of grain. I thought of Anna in this same scene, being dragged away from the bar, her shoes grating against the late-night asphalt, everything becoming fuzzy, just wanting to go home and sleep. They walked past my pickup truck and stopped twenty or so feet away, in front of Simon's red Mazda. His sports car in the shadows. I reached into the back of my truck and grabbed the rebar. Simon leaned the girl against the car and reached into his pocket for the keys.

I snuck up slowly, heart pounding, grateful for the shadows, watching him unlock the passenger door. He leaned over to place the girl in the seat and stood back up. He shut the passenger door, began to turn around, and that's when I slammed the rebar into the back of his neck. Hard. Right into that date-raping, punk-ass bull neck of his. Don't try that shit in my fucking land! With my fucking woman!

At first, there wasn't any blood. He just lay there, head on the pavement, gasping for air, hands open against the ground, clutching at the tar for breath. I stood over him, adrenaline surging, drenched in the night's filthy humidity, ready with the rebar for another blow. The fucking pig. Eat my fucking rebar.

Then I saw the blood. Small red rivulets at the corner of his mouth, dripping and spraying and bubbling to the ground with each exaggerated gasp. I turned, looked over at the girl. She shook her head back and forth against the headrest, whimpering, slurring incoherently. I rushed over and touched her shoulder through the open window, told her that everything was going to be fine. She was safe now. She half opened her eyes and looked at my hand on her shoulder, batted at it uselessly, then dropped both arms into her lap and passed out.

I turned back to Simon. He gave two great belly-deep dry heaves and went quiet. I grabbed him by the wrists and dragged him to my pickup truck. He made dry, croaking vomiting sounds as I hoisted him up the side of the truck and pushed him into the open bed. His blood soaked my tan t-shirt. I grabbed the rebar from the ground and threw it in the back of the pickup with Simon. I ran over to his car and saw that the girl was breathing heavy and deep, her mouth open, her arms dangling at her sides. I rolled up the windows, locked the doors, and ran back to my truck. Simon was motionless in the cab. I headed back to Swans for help.

***

Jasper clutched a rifle as he unlatched the door. It was 3:30 in the morning. I was covered in blood and Simon lay at the end of the driveway where I'd managed to drag him up from the dock. I spoke to Jasper through the screen door, told him what had happened, who Simon was. He lit a cigarette and listened, propped the rifle against the door frame. I spoke quickly. A small army of insects formed against the screen, beating themselves against the mesh, throbbing and buzzing for light. Jasper scratched the back of his head and exhaled slowly.

—We gotta get Eddie.

Jasper came outside and leaned over Simon, rolled him onto his stomach. He fished a wallet out of his back pocket and opened it, studied it for a while.

—Get him back to the boat.

***

Ten minutes later Eddie jogged up the driveway in a tank top and sweatpants. I stood in the light of Jasper's house and Eddie saw that I was covered in blood. He stopped in front of me and said fuck over and over while shaking his head. Jasper gave Eddie a whistle from the porch and tossed him the wallet. Eddie caught it but didn't open it.

—Get a few cinder blocks and some rope.

Eddie disappeared into the shed and Jasper walked back to the doorway to grab his rifle and shut the screen door. Eddie came back from the shed with two large cinder blocks and a loop of rope around his chest. I stood shifting on my feet in the moonlight, not knowing what to do, how to be helpful at resolving this impossible mess. Jasper walked up next to me and held out his hand.

—You stay here.

Without looking him in the eyes, I reached into my pocket and put the keys in his hand. A few minutes later I heard the engine start up down by the dock and had a desperate urge to call Anna, tell her that it was done, that I'd gotten revenge. Instead I just stood there dumbly in the night, at the edge of Jasper's yard, mosquitoes gnawing at my flesh, suddenly exhausted and sad, wondering what would come next.[35]

---

[35]Marsh informed me via email that he began working on this first chapter ("The South African") with only a vague notion of where to take the story after Jasper and Eddie leave with Simon's body. He wanted to capture the complications associated with such acts of vigilante-style, small town justice, and he considered writing a second chapter from Jasper's point of view, starting at the point when the narrator appears at his door. However, Marsh said that he struggled with this second chapter because he couldn't match the raw intensity of the narrator's voice, and he felt like the remainder of the novel would simply revolve around the violent climax that occurred in the first chapter. He ultimately gave up on the novel altogether, though he did use this same narrative voice for several chapters of his unpublished novel *Sensual Nomads*.

Selection #7 — Bird Count[36]
Metinic Island
Frank Hamilton
29 August 1986

It is a common phenomenon for individuals and small groups to head to Maine islands in search of meaning, inspiration, or solitude. Such a raw, rugged, and remote landscape seems to draw out a meditative, contemplative spirit in many visitors by removing them, both physically and psychologically, from the many distractions one finds in life on the mainland. For many individuals, there is a certain restorative and therapeutic power, almost bordering on the mystical, to venturing offshore and immersing oneself in a unique ecosystem shaped so powerfully by the surrounding sea.

This selection, written by Frank Hamilton in the form of a letter to his two sons, provides an account of one man's inner journey as he spends ten days on Metinic Island assisting with an Arctic tern restoration project[37] for the Maine Audubon Society. Metinic is a secluded, undeveloped island, and though it is clear that Frank did not necessarily go there with soul-searching intentions, he is nonetheless thrust into a Zen-like

---

[36]This submission has been analyzed extensively from an ecocritical perspective by Dr. Samantha Friedlander from Unity College in her paper entitled "The Interiority of Outdoor Experience: An Island Files Case Study from Metinic Island" in *North American Studies in Literature and the Environment (ISLE)*, University of Nevada, Reno, Vol. 7, 1985. Ecocriticism, in essence, is the study of the relationship between literature and the environment. I would recommend this paper by Dr. Friedlander to anyone interested in learning more about how to interpret literature from an earth-centered approach.

experience in which he must confront and wrestle with the demons of his past.

A three-generation resident of Islesboro Island, Frank made four submissions to the Island Society from 1983–1986. His submissions begin shortly after his wife passed away in February 1983, and seven months after his retirement. His first three submissions include routine community information and anecdotes and do not appear elsewhere in this volume. What is notable about Frank's fourth and final submission is how deeply introspective and personal it is, and how it offers a complete stylistic and structural departure from his previous submissions. It is also interesting to consider why Frank would submit a letter to the Island Society that is intended for his sons and that is so personal and oftentimes painful in nature. Though Frank passed away in 1989 and there is no way of truly understanding his rationale behind this submission, it is important to note that the Island Files regularly served as a sort of repository for members' personal reflections, stories, opinions, or ideas.

As a maritime engineer[38] for Meuller Shipping Company, the majority of Frank Hamilton's adult life was spent at sea. Like my own father who worked for the Merchant Marines,

---

[37]Arctic terns are known for having the longest annual migratory journey of any bird, often traveling upwards of 40,000 miles per year on their convoluted route from the Arctic to the Antarctic coasts. Due to concern about declining tern populations off the Maine coast in the early 1980s, several groups, including the Maine Audubon Society, began programs to rehabilitate and protect these populations. Researchers on several Maine islands reported a significant increase in Arctic tern populations through the 1990s and early 2000s, though a 2015 article from the Island Institute reports that all Maine seabird populations are on the decline.

[38]Frank graduated from Maine Maritime Academy with an engineering degree in 1954.

Frank would spend six to seven months deployed on a freighter, followed by a one to two month leave at home. Such long periods of absence often prove challenging for family dynamics, and in Frank's case this tension was compounded by his rough physical nature, heavy drinking, and rumored womanizing. He alludes to this behavior in his letter, and even gives several specific examples of memories that continue to haunt him, though the measured, articulate, and thoughtful tone of this submission stands in marked contrast to this behavior.

When I first considered including Frank's submission in this volume I reached out via email to Frank's sons, Aaron and Jonathan. Only Aaron responded to my query and said that neither he nor his brother ever received a letter from their father. I offered to forward him a digital copy of the letter but he declined, saying that he was busy and did not want to revisit that chapter of his life. He did give me his blessing to use the letter for this volume under the condition that I change names in order to protect privacy.

Metinic Island still serves as an important migratory pitstop and nesting grounds for many seabirds, including over a thousand Arctic terns. The U.S. Fish & Wildlife Service now operates the seabird sanctuary program and stations interns on the island during the seabird nesting season from April 1 through August 31.

***

Joshua Anchors

Dear Aaron and Jonathan,

I'm writing this to you from behind my bird blind in a large field on Metinic Island, a narrow strip of land six miles off-shore with just a few structures and no year-round residents. The island is mostly a long stretch of grass and granite, with a patch of forest in the middle where the dormitory and mess hall are located. For the past nine days I've been here volunteering on a migratory bird counting project, something I never imagined myself doing. I've never been a birdwatcher, and I don't know much at all about birds, but my friend Max has done this for the past three years and said that all I have to do is keep my eyes open and take notes in my field journal. Max and I shared a bunkbed in a big dorm room with two serious birdwatchers from Orono, George and Tim. The four of us eat breakfast together every morning and then split up and sit behind our blinds until lunchtime, taking notes on how many terns or eiders or warblers we see and what they're doing. Sometimes we see sheep from the other side of the island and we put that in our notes, too. After lunch we go back out for four hours and do the same thing. When Max first proposed this idea I thought it sounded like a ridiculous way to spend ten days and I couldn't believe he thought it would be good for me, but then I thought what the hell else would I be doing with my time if I were at home. Watching television and eating ice cream? Puttering around the house? Sitting alone on the porch watching the lobster boats go by?

When we first arrived out here, Max told me that the toughest part of this job is being out behind the blind for seven or eight hours a day, especially if there isn't much bird action. He said that's a lot of time for anyone to spend alone on a small island in the middle of the ocean. That's the reason he invited me, though, because he thought a change of scenery and some time without the usual distractions would do me good. He said it worked wonders for him a few years back when he was going through a dark spell, and he knows me well enough to tell that I've been going through that same kind of spell.

All I can say is that these past few years I've been thinking a lot about you both and how we've lost touch. I know I made a ton of mistakes over the years and I don't blame you one bit for not wanting to see me. The last year or so I've been wondering if either of you could ever forgive me, but as soon as I think about reaching out I start remembering all the ways I let you and your mother down. Those are the stories that just keep circling around in my brain. Last year I wrote a long letter to you both but threw it in the woodstove. I guess I just didn't want to get hurt by not hearing back from you. Even though I've been sober for thirteen months and have changed a lot since you were boys (I quit smoking, too), I figured that you'd only remember the old me. Until now, I think I just didn't have the courage to reach out and try. One day a few months back, Max told me I was digging my own grave if I stayed home for much longer beating myself up and wallowing in regret. That's when he invited me out here.

I've sure had some ups and downs over these past ten days. It started off like magic that first day because everything was new and there was so much to learn. It's also beautiful and peaceful out here, without all the tourist bustle that you find on Islesboro during the summer. I spent most of that first day focused on a bunch of little tasks – fixing the camp chair, tightening the mesh blind, studying the nautical chart for the area around Metinic—that made the time pass and gave my hands something to do. You may remember, but one good thing about me is that I've always been pretty handy, and I like to keep busy. By the end of that first day, though, I'd finished up all my chores by 4:30 p.m. and spent the last thirty minutes almost in a panic, wondering what I'd do with myself the next nine days now that I was settled in.

I remember that second morning I woke up and everything was so still and quiet and I dreaded the thought of going out to my blind. I didn't want to have to just sit there with myself all day, all those stories running through my mind with nothing to do. It seemed like I was putting myself through torture. I looked for Max but he was probably out reading somewhere, and I knew that George and Tim were out on their early morning birdwatching walk, so that left me all alone. I couldn't even turn on the radio or the tv for company like I would of at home.

I don't know how, but thanks to some miracle I pushed through those second and third days. I tried to make myself interested in the birds, but I couldn't get into them even after George gave me a big lecture about how amazing they are. My legs and butt hurt and I shifted in my camp chair every minute or so. When the ranger, Ian, stopped by during his morning rounds he must have thought I was a madman or a chatterbox because I was so happy to have a distraction that I wouldn't stop talking. After Ian left on those mornings, the stillness seemed like it was suffocating me. The sound of my wheezy breath drowned out all the other noises. I'd start thinking about the time when you boys were young or when your mother was sick, and as soon as those thoughts came up I'd start sweating behind my blind. It was goddam pitiful.

I waited until lunch on the fourth day to tell Max that I wanted to leave. I just couldn't face another afternoon out there. The idea of getting off Metinic and back to my regular life with all its dumb distractions made me feel light-headed, like I was being released from months of solitary confinement. It took a lot for me to have that conversation with Max because it made me feel like a quitter and a loser, like I couldn't hack it out here with the birds. Max didn't try to convince me to stay. He said the next boat off the island was the next morning at 11:00 and that I should tell Ian at dinner.

The afternoon of that fourth day wasn't too bad now that the end was in sight. Funny how that works. I knew I'd be back at home soon with plenty to keep me busy, or at least distracted. Somehow everything just seemed better that afternoon. My legs hurt less. I saw a tern chick wobble over the rocks. The weather cooled down and a nice salt breeze blew over my station. That evening at dinner Max asked me if I thought I could last another day so that Ian would have time to send for another volunteer.

Max and I took a long walk that evening along the north end of Metinic and that's when he suggested that I write this letter. He said that I needed to move forward and stop living in the past, otherwise I'd just feel guilty for the rest of my life and what good would that do me. A letter to you boys would at least give me the chance to be honest about the past and show you that I've changed. Max told me not to expect a miracle from just one letter, and he's right. One letter can't make up for a lifetime of mistakes, and I don't expect you to forgive me or want to see me again just because I'm reaching out now. Like Max said, at least this will give me something productive to do and think about during the day instead of getting caught up in memories that just make me feel guilty.

When Ian checked in with me during his rounds on my fifth morning, I told him that I was going to stay. It made me feel good to tell him that. Even though I dreaded the thought of five more days out here, now at least I had a goal in mind, something to work towards. I could think about what I wanted to say to you boys <u>in the present</u> instead of just remembering all the ways I'd let you down. That afternoon I started writing down notes in the back of my field journal, all the thoughts and stories and memories that passed through my mind that needed to be in this letter.

At dinner that evening Ian surprised us by bringing out a half-gallon of chocolate ice cream to celebrate the half-way point of our time on Metinic. We sat at our picnic table and ate the ice cream and told stories and it was a beautiful evening. I remember George told a story about the time he volunteered for some kind of puffin project on Eastern Egg Rock and over the course of a few weeks he watched as a real puffin fell in love with a wooden decoy puffin. He said that the real puffin would cuddle with the decoy, rub against it, speak to it, and sometimes bring it a fresh-caught fish. The tough part, he said, was that when it came time for the puffins to migrate south for the winter the real puffin didn't want to leave behind the decoy. Max joked that his second wife might as well have been a decoy, and we all thought that was a pretty good one. I was real glad to be out there that evening.

Now I felt like I was on some kind of a mission when I sat behind the blind. I wrote down everything, the big stuff and the little stuff, it didn't matter. I wanted it all. I dug into the dark corners of my brain to get at it, and I found a lot, stories and memories I hadn't thought about for years. It felt good to get it out on paper. I imagined writing you a long letter that listed all of my mistakes. A sort of catalogue of my failures, just for the record. I didn't want you to think I was hiding any-thing. I wanted it all out on the table. I felt like that was the only way I could truly own it and apologize for it. I started writ-ing that letter on my seventh day and it made the time pass. I've never been to therapy before, unless you call AA therapy, but from what Max tells me I bet going to therapy is kind of like writing that letter because it gave me the chance to get out in the open a bunch of things I'd been holding onto in my mind for an awful long time.

Of all the images that have been playing over and over in my mind these past few days, one of the images that bothers me the most is one I have of you, Jonathan, standing on the back porch in the twilight, your head covered in red spaghetti sauce, strands of angel hair pasta stuck in your hair, looking up at me with rage. I remember I'd only been home for two or three days after seven months at sea and one of the first things I do is get drunk and throw a bowl of pasta at my oldest son because of a broken lawnmower or something. This is the kind of image that haunts me, and I'm writing it down here because I want you to know that it haunts me. Maybe that makes you feel better, maybe it doesn't, but it's important for me to put that image out there and own up to it.

There's also one scene with you, Aaron, that's been nag-ging at me particularly hard since I got to Metinic. You were posing for a photo with three of your friends after the high school graduation ceremony, all smiles and laughter, decked out in your caps and gowns, and then you saw me coming, probably staggering, from across the lawn. We made eye contact for a split second and you turned away and led your friends back into the auditorium. I felt so shameful that morning for missing the ceremony, on top of all the other things I'd missed for stupid reasons, and I could feel your hate and disappointment deep in my bones as our eyes met and your face turned serious. I knew I'd already lost your brother, but I think that was the moment I knew down deep that I'd lost you both.

Ian stopped by my blind on the morning of my ninth day and I told him I was using all the down time out here to write a letter to my boys. He asked a few questions about you both and then told me that he and his wife write a letter to their daughter every month. She lives in Maryland and they only see her once a year, usually for Christmas, so the letters help them stay in touch. I noticed a swarm of Arctic terns burst into the sky from the nearby rocks while he was talking and I pointed up at them. We saw a lone Herring gull cruising above the shore and Ian said it was probably on the hunt for tern chicks and eggs. We heard the terns screeching and screaming as they mobbed the gull, swarming around it to defend their young. I can't explain it, but something shifted in me in that moment and I knew that needed to send a different letter than the one I'd been working on. That might have been the letter that I needed to write, but not the one that you needed to read. No need to make you two relive all those memories just so I can get some therapy. Max told me later that writing is sometimes like that, you work hard on something that you think is a good idea and then you suddenly realize that it's not a good idea and you have to move in a whole new direction.

Now it's my tenth and final day out here and I've got a half hour left behind the blind to wrap this up. I'll be glad to get back home, but I've got to admit that I've had some good moments on Metinic, especially after I made it through those first few days.

I can't say that I'll miss the birds that much, though I do keep thinking about what George said the other night at dinner about my career on the freighter being similar to a tern's life because we both cover so many miles across the sea. I only wish I had used my stopovers at home to take care of my young like they do. If there's any lesson the terns have taught me, that's the one: time on land is precious, spend it wisely, don't waste it on stupid shit.

Even if nothing else comes from my birdwatching days out here, I hope this letter at least gives you some peace of mind in knowing that your wicked old pa on Islesboro is thinking about you and loves you. In the end, that's all I really mean to say here. The rest, I suppose, can go to the birds.

Sincerely,

Frank

Selection #8—Final Jeopardy
Squirrel Island, Boothbay Harbor
Constance Moody[39]
18 June 1987

One of the fascinating socio-cultural dynamics that shapes the culture of many Maine island communities is the coexistence of working-class native islanders alongside more affluent temporary residents who are often referred to as "summer people." While this longstanding co-existence may fuel a mild undercurrent of class tension in some communities, it also creates a powerful co-dependency between the two groups in that each relies on the other for either services, labor, support, or money. Given this inter-connection, many summer people, especially those who have visited a particular island for multiple generations, are well-integrated into the fabric of island life, understand island culture and history, and are subject to all the informal rules, rituals, and customs that come with being part of a small, tightly-knit community.

This brief selection makes reference to a rather comical community episode in which longtime Squirrel Island summer resident, Dick Jensen, blows a $4200 lead on the game show Jeopardy in June 1987. A tenured professor of history at Boston College, Dick was dominant throughout the first two rounds of the show and ultimately wagered his entire pot on the category American Geography during Final Jeopardy. Local television ratings suggest that many coastal Maine residents tuned into

---

[39]One of Constance Moody's submissions is also included as a sample selection in the introduction to this volume.

the show that evening to support Dick, an honorary if not native Mainer, and Squirrel Islanders took particular pride in having a local chosen for thirty minutes in the national spotlight. However, when host Alex Trebek read the final clue, "This state boasts the longest coastline on the Atlantic Coast," Dick responded by writing down "Florida." The answer, of course, is Maine.[40]

I visited Dick at his home on Squirrel Island in June 2017 and spoke with him about his appearance on Jeopardy thirty years earlier. Now retired, Dick lives full-time on the island and said, all in good humor, that in the end his disastrous mistake on Jeopardy actually made him feel more a part of the island community and, for better or worse, cemented his place in local folklore. "They'll never let me live that one down," Dick said. "To this day I still get an occasional Florida joke or someone asking me if I need to borrow $4200." He said that in a strange way it was good for islanders to see him mess up so royally and so publicly. "I think summer people can sometimes seem invulnerable or snobbish with all their money and education. What happened on Jeopardy kind of humanized me in a way that was really valuable for making me part of this community."

The author of this selection, Constance Moody,[41] made 96 submissions to the Island Files from 1981–1989. All of her submissions come in the form of brief, informal letters that offer a

---

[40]According to a National Oceanic and Atmospheric Administration (NOAA) report entitled <u>Shoreline Mileage of the United States</u>, Maine has 3,478 miles of coastline while Florida has 3,341 on the Atlantic Coast. Florida does indeed have a longer coastline than Maine, with a total of 8,436 miles, though 5,095 of those miles are on the Gulf Coast.

[41]Her maiden name is Castonguay, a common French-Canadian surname in the paper mill towns of western and northern Maine.

general recap of her month and any pertinent undertakings. Constance, who grew up in a large French Catholic family on Cousins Island, only attended school until the eighth grade at the Cousins' one-room schoolhouse. She married fisherman Charles Moody when she was sixteen-years-old and moved to Squirrel Island. When both Charles and Constance passed away in 2007 and 2010, respectively, Dick Jensen attended their wakes.

***

Dear MWIS,

Here all is well except for using some bad words when I look at the lawn all full of mole hills what a mess and this morning there are 10 deers in my back lawn. I felt like shooting one and having fresh meat for dinner. Heh. Had some nice weather this month for Carson's graduation party but it was cool outside in the shade and I wore my sweater the hole day. Can you believe it in the month of June! There was a mass at the cementry at 1:00 yesterday afternoon that I went to and then the three matantes[42] and Ethel came over to eat supper. We ate the jello salad and chicken. No leftovers which is the way I like it!

Well this is news now that I think of it! That man Dick who lives out here summers well he was on that game show Jeopardy last week and boy o boy did he make a bad guess from what Tony says. Lost all his money on that last question. And all he had to say was Maine! Imagine that! I don't watch that show usually but Tony called me up and told me that that man from down the street was on tv so I turned it on. That host he asked those questions so fast I couldn't keep up! I don't know how anybody can know that much they must have studied real hard at school. Heh.

Much for now.
God Bless.
Connie

---

[42]Constance uses the colloquial French-Canadian term *"matante"* (my aunt) to refer to her three sisters who never married and still live together on the family farm.

Selection #9—Swept to Sea
Andrews Island—Frenchman Bay
Arnetta Sidwell
28 July 1996

The qualities of toughness and grit that are often attributed to native islanders have much to do with the harshness of the landscape in which they dwell. Even on its most agreeable days, the Maine Coast is an environment steeped in risk – strong currents, frigid waters, rogue waves, the rapid onset of dense fog or strong winds. This is an environment that takes lives every year, especially during the summer months when visitors either underestimate these risks or when conditions can change so rapidly that even experienced outdoorspeople can be tested.

This selection captures the tragic aftermath of one kayaker, Jack Baptiste, who was swept out to sea in the summer of 1996. A southern Maine native and longtime summer resident of Andrews Island, Jack was, by all accounts, a skilled sea kayaker who simply made an ill-advised decision to launch in heavy fog on the morning of July 25, 1996.

There are two distinct features that make this selection so unique. First, it captures to what extent the Baptiste family had truly become integrated into island life during their eighteen years as summer residents. Second, it brings in the story of Martin Acton who struggled for many years with the 1984 loss of his twin brother in a fishing accident around Platt's Bank. In the simplest of terms and in the plainest of language, Mrs. Arnetta Sidwell writes about these losses and the psychological ripple-effects they have on a small island community.

Ed and Helen Baptiste originally visited Andrews Island in 1979 and claim to have fallen in love with it immediately. In

1980, they purchased Will Gallant's house on the northwest end and began renovating it the following summer. From 1981– 1995, they brought both of their boys, Jack and Murdoch, to the island for the months of July and August. During these years, members of the Baptiste family are mentioned by name at least three times in the Island Files.[43] The tragic death of Helen Baptiste in a car crash in 1995 is not noted in the Island Files, though Mrs. Sidwell does refer to "the need for prayer in these very sad times" in her September 1995 submission.

Reading the selection below, it is evident to what extent the Baptiste family, though originally visitors to the island, had woven their lives into the fabric of this tight-knit community. One telling sign of this is the impact that Jack's loss has on Martin Acton. Ever since the loss of his own brother in 1984, Martin suffered from short but intense bouts of depression in the face of community tragedies, especially when accidents befell those close to him. Otherwise known as a gregarious, fun-loving man, Martin once pranked Ed Baptiste by stuffing one of his lobster traps with Barbie Dolls and phallic paraphernalia.

Mrs. Arnetta Sidwell, the author of this selection, is the proprietor of On The Rocks, a small general store and coffee shop overlooking the harbor where a group of fishermen congregate to drink coffee every morning before heading out to their

----

[43]Files submissions pertaining to the Baptiste family:

Harry Owens, 1984: "Ed Baptiste got his recreational lobster license and set out his traps over by The Neck."

Harry Owens, 1989: "One of the Baptiste boys broke his leg playing by the cliffs and Jim Anderberg had to take him to the mainland late at night to go to the hospital. They say he might have also punctured a lung as well."

Arnetta Sidwell, 1993: "Got a call from Helen Baptiste this month with word that Ed passed away. Won't be the same without him around in the summers. I'll talk with the Daughters of Isabella about sending over some flowers to the family."

boats. She retired in 2008 and the store is now owned and operated by her nephew, Paul Sidwell. Included below is the Camden Herald newspaper clipping that Mrs. Sidwell included in her original submission and provides more detailed context on the loss of Jack Baptiste.

***

"Longtime Andrews Island Summer Resident Swept
to Sea in Kayak"
The Camden Herald
July 28, 1996

After an exhaustive search of Frenchman Bay and surrounding areas over the past forty-eight hours, the U.S. Coast Guard and the Maine Inland Fisheries & Wildlife report that they are suspending the search for Cape Elizabeth native and longtime Andrews Island summer resident Jack Baptiste.

"At this point we have reason to believe that Mr. Baptiste may have been swept out to sea on the morning of July 26," said Capt. Dennis Brady, Commander of the Coast Guard Sector Northern New England. "That was a morning of dense fog that gave way to heavy southeast winds. Those conditions would have disoriented even the most experienced kayaker."

Mr. Baptiste was reported missing on the afternoon of July 26 from Andrews Island, where he was stay-ing in the family cottage with his brother, Murdoch Baptiste, and several friends. According to Tina Wu, one of the friends who had joined the Baptiste brothers on the island, "We saw that he wasn't there around 10:00 a.m. but we didn't report it

until about three hours later when we saw that a
kayak was missing from the dock.[44]

Jack Baptiste attended Cape Elizabeth High School
and received a BA in International Relations at Tufts
University in 1992. He had spent the last four years
working as a research assistant for the non-profit
organization Partners in Health, dividing his time
between Port-au-Prince, Haiti, and Boston,
Massachusetts. His wife, Jasmine, was unavailable
for comment at the time of this printing.

***

On everybody's minds these days is the loss of our Jack (I'll
let the article I clipped out speak for itself), and of course how
no one can believe it and so soon after Helen. How much does
one family have to suffer? Doesn't seem right, but the Good
Lord works in mysterious ways and I've always thought that.

Martin stopped in this morning finally, though he didn't
stick around to talk to the boys like he normally would. Just
grabbed his coffee and headed out to his boat. We're all wor-

---

[44]Based on a December 2015 interview with Tina Wu I learned that
the brothers had initially planned the island outing together in order
to sprinkle their mother's ashes into the sea, per her request.
According to Ms. Wu, Jack was unaware that Murdoch had invited
other friends along for the trip and was furious. "I think Jack thought
he was just going to the island with his brother to sprinkle their
mothers' ashes. An intimate sort of family thing. He didn't know that
Murdoch had invited us, and I think that's why they got into a big
fight that night. I felt really bad about the whole thing, and then of
course the next afternoon it got totally crazy when we figured out
Jack was missing."

ried about him naturally, but in a few days, he'll be back to his old self, joking and annoying everybody with all his morning energy (Lord only knows where he gets it, the guy must wake up whistling I swear), and I'll be glad for it. These boys aren't the funnest bunch to be around without Martin and his chatter! Wakes me up, gives me a good laugh most days. Anyway, Carl was up to the post office yesterday and ran into Judy who says he'll be all right and that we shouldn't worry and that he just needs to be left alone for a bit. She should know, I guess, but I'll give her a little buzz tonight and see if she needs anything or maybe see if she wants to get out of the house at least, maybe play some cards over to Betsy's. Almost a week now since the news came...can't imagine how she does it, especially now that the kids are grown and gone. A whole week without a peep from him. Enough to drive a person crazy. Would drive me crazy anyway.

Well, it seems weird to go into other news from here, given how it all would seem pretty small compared to this. So I'll just end here and ask whoever reads this to say a prayer for poor Murdoch. The only one left of that family, poor boy! And of course say a prayer for Martin and his family, too. Seems as though they could use it just as much. Maybe more.

God Bless,
Arnetta S.

Selection #10—The Hermit
Manana Island—Muscongus Bay
Kathleen White
25 October 2001

Maine islands present a certain paradox for those seeking refuge from the larger world. On the one hand, many islands are relatively isolated, sparsely populated, and difficult to access —ideal qualities for anyone seeking seclusion. On the other hand, as Philip Conkling writes in Islands in Time, "The last place you should go to get away from your neighbors is an island community. City folk can choose to be anonymous and invisible; island folk never can. To be a hermit, you need your own island."[45]

The central character in this submission, Captain Ray Phillips, did just that in his quest for solitude: he found his own island. Widely known as the Hermit of Manana,[46] Phillips lived alone for nearly fifty years, from 1928 through 1975, in a small cottage built of driftwood on rocky and windswept Manana Island.

Twelve miles off the mainland, Manana is neighbors with the popular Monhegan Island, well-known as a sanctuary for artists because of its picturesque landscape and idyllic atmosphere. Phillips lived a tranquil yet relatively sociable existence on Manana, chatting for hours with visitors, rowing to Monhegan once a week for mail and supplies, and visiting a

---

[45]*Islands in Time.* Third Edition, 2011, Page 293.

[46]The New York Times obituary, <u>"Ray Philips, Celebrated Hermit of Maine Coast Island, Is Dead,"</u> provides detailed information on Phillips' life and background.

small town on the mainland several times a year to get his hair and beard trimmed. Neither a recluse nor insane, Phillips often told people that he simply opted for a simple, quiet life after spending his earlier years in the US Army and working in Manhattan.

In April 2001, the Monhegan Museum[47] put on a small exhibit honoring the life of Ray Phillips. This is where the author of this submission, Adèle Saint-Pierre, a musician and educator from Jay, Maine, first learned about the Hermit of Manana and was inspired to write a song about him. During Adèle's three-day trip to Monhegan in the summer of 2001, she stayed with her former college roommate, Kathleen White, a two-generation native of Monhegan. Adèle wrote the song "Manana" several weeks after this trip and sent the lyrics and a recording of the song on CD to Kathleen in September 2001. The following month Kathleen submitted the lyrics and a copy of the CD to the Island Society. She has two other submissions in the Island Files, one short poem that appears in Volume II, and one detailed account of the community's successful day-long search for Jim Peddie, a lobsterman from the nearby town of Friendship who became lost at sea during a storm.

"Manana" is the only song submission in the Island Files and the only submission with an accompanying audio recording.[48] I strongly recommend that readers listen to this song in addition to reading the lyrics as it will add another dimension to the experience and meaning. Also included after the song lyrics is an email interview I conducted with Adèle in May 2018 in which she provides analysis and interpretation of the song. Adèle now works as a French and Spanish teacher at a private school in Brooklyn and has not visited Manana since 2001.

***

---

[47]https://monheganmuseum.org

Manana
By Adèle Saint-Pierre

In the dark
the path we cut
through fog like whispers raining.

Mother Rock, Father Sea
your love was never waning.

When we crossed the hundred yards
another world awaited.
Was it here what you sought from life?

And you wrestled with your demons,
memories replanted
in the weeds
and the rock
of this island.

Did it seem the thousandth time
your feet had never wandered

the same old trail?
It never fails
the heart it often blunders.

But like a root
you clung to the bowels of this island.
For all my travels
you knew more than I.

And you danced with the fog
in her white dress.
Secret vows in silence

linger now in the dark
of this island.

If you crown your head in smoke
will you have to answer?
To your own history
oh shepherd do you wonder?

A simple state
you retreat to the shadows of this island.
With little trace
so you left this life

And the lantern that you lighted
flickered, then united
in the dark
and the night
of this island.

Will the truth of the life you pondered
echo in the yonder?
Or will it go unspoken?
Or will it go unspoken?
Or will it go unspoken?

---

[48]Access the Manana audio recording via this link (https://www.youtube.com/watch?v=vu2qROabTXA) or go to YouTube.com and type in Manana Adele Saint Pierre.

Email Interview with Adèle Saint-Pierre
May 2018

What inspired you to write this song?
A feeling of desolation when I imagined being alone on the island at night, wondering why anybody would voluntarily choose that kind of solitary life. It was an intense feeling, and it kind of scared me at the time. It made me want to immediately row back to Monhegan with Kathy and go somewhere well-lit and warm and have a rum and coke surrounded by a bunch of people talking and laughing. I vaguely remember a feeling of being lost at sea, deeply alone, scared that I would not find my way back to humanity.

There is a haunting quality to the mood and rhythm of this song. Can you talk about the process you used for choosing that particular mood?
The entire experience of visiting and learning about Manana was haunting for me, so that quality just naturally infused my songwriting. My musical partner at the time, Jason,[49] was brilliant enough to come up with a rhythm that perfectly captured the mysterious and haunting quality of my experience.

In the line, "And you wrestled with your demons," what "demons" do you believe the protagonist is wrestling with?
I can only imagine. I leave this to listeners to interpret as they wish. What demons would drive someone to live with a flock of sheep on a remote island in Maine? However, maybe demons play no role in his story, maybe he is like an ascetic monk seeking spiritual enlightenment through self-deprivation and isolation. But I don't know, some sort of demon seems pretty likely.

---

[49]Jason Mancine: https://www.mancine.net/?page_id=8

Can you discuss the meaning of the line, "And you danced with the fog in her white dress?"
I remember one photo from the exhibition where he is feeding goats or sheep (or maybe it was geese?) by his cabin, and I remember thinking how this one photo made him seem Jesus-like or at least priest-like in the sense that he had given up all his worldly possessions to live alone in communion with nature. The hermit, like Jesus (at least so the Bible says), is chaste. In moving out to Manana and giving up worldly possessions, he also renounces sexual relations and the opportunity to have children. The "fog in her white dress" is nature, the hermit "dances" with her on their wedding day, as the idea of "secret vows in silence" in the next line suggest.

Selection #11 — Kyriacos
Monhegan & Manana Islands — Muscongus Bay
Evelyn "Evie" Reed
July 1996 – April 1997

Maine island communities are known for their tightly-knit social networks that often react to outsiders with a wary sense of both guardedness and curiosity. The inner workings and authentic character of these communities thus seems inaccessible to most outsiders, especially those who visit only in the temperate summer months. Life on a Maine island can be tough, after all, and requires sacrifice, suffering, grit, and resilience. Understandably, those who live the intense joys and hardships of this life are not inclined to simply open their doors, and certainly not their hearts, to any newcomer who moves in. These are privileges that must be earned. Yet this collective guardedness, this holding of outsiders at a distance, exists for another, more unassuming, reason: the need to avoid getting attached, emotionally or otherwise, to those who will inevitably leave. Just as much as this guardedness is a form of mistrust or skepticism of the outside world, it is also a form of self-protection and communal survival.

This selection poignantly captures the complications and delights of a friendship between native Monhegan islander Evelyn Reed and temporary resident Kyriacos Kazantzakis. This friendship evolves over the course of Kyriacos' ten month stay on neighboring Manana Island and is documented by Evelyn through her monthly Island Files submissions. Though it is unlikely that Evelyn intended to tell the story of this friendship through her submissions, a clear narrative arc emerges when the excerpts concerning Kyriacos are compiled in chronological order. In this selection, I have included every reference to

Kyriacos that appears in Evelyn's thirty-nine handwritten pages of submissions from July 1996 to April 1997.

As the most prolific contributor to the Island Files with 117 submissions from 1979 to 1998, Evelyn Reed wrote a form of running commentary most months that included a combination of island gossip, personal observations, and updates on community affairs. Her submissions typically do not focus on storytelling in a traditional sense, but rather move quickly from topic to topic, allowing her to cover a broad range of subjects over several pages.

Evelyn Reed served as head librarian at the Monhegan Memorial Library from 1974 to 1998 and wrote most of her submissions while behind the library desk. The library served as one of the essential social hubs on the island, especially during summers, and Evelyn gleaned a significant amount of material for her submissions from speaking with library guests and exchanging gossip at the checkout counter. Evelyn retired from the library in 1998 and passed away in 2006. Her husband Randy lives in a retirement home in Bucksport, while their two boys, Cole and Curtis, have relocated from Monhegan to the Ellsworth area.

Kyriacos was born in Nicosia, Cyprus, and raised in Belfast, Maine, where his parents owned the popular Greek restaurant, Kathodon, from 1982 to 1996. He now works as a history teacher at a private school in Charleston, South Carolina. He did not respond to several attempts to reach him via email.

***

July 1996

Well Ray's[50] old mansion on Manana will finally get a polish! Who knows why he wants to go through all the trouble, but a young guy came out the other day and set up in the shack. Of course he had to get Jack's[51] permission first, but why would Jack say no to anyone wanting to fix up that eyesore for free. Hasn't really been used since Ray passed back in 1975 so this guy's got his work cut out for him.

...

That guy living on Manana will be working at the Trailing Yew for the summer, so I hear. When lobster season starts he'll be sternman for Buddy Webster out on the *Griffin*. Marjorie says he's a writer which explains why he wants to live out on Manana for some peace and quiet. Seems like everyone who comes out here in the summer is either a painter a photographer or a writer, so nothing new there. He paid down for Linda's rowboat for the full year so it looks like he wants to stick with Manana...just wonder if he'll be so sure about that when winter comes!

...

---

[50]Captain Ray Phillips, commonly known as the Hermit of Manana. See "Submission #10—Manana" for more information about his life and background.

[51]Jack Eagleton, Monhegan Constable from 1993–1999.

The new guy stopped by the library this morning and told me his name is Kyriacos. The only reason I know how to spell it is because he wanted to get a book but we didn't have it so I ordered it from Augusta and had to write down his name on the request form. First time I've ever heard a name like that. He told me it's Greek but he grew up in Belfast so he's not really Greek I guess. Real polite young man and good looking. Linda came in after he left and said that I'd found myself a real catch. As if!

August 1996

Who knew Kyriacos could play the piano? The ferry delivered Edna's piano the other day and he started playing it in the back of Jim's pickup as soon as they had it loaded. He sat right on a lobster trap and played music while Jim drove real slow. Right in the back of the pickup! They went all the way to Edna's like that, all the way to the end of Deadman's Cove! I heard them coming up Main Street from a ways off so I poked my head out of the library to see what was the commotion. Kyriacos saw me and gave me a big wave. Jim was slapping the side of his truck and it was quite a ruckus. But a good one. I think I even saw Ellen smile for once when she caught sight of it. I heard that Edna wasn't too happy about all of it at first, though Jim told everyone that Kyriacos "sweet talked" himself out of any trouble pretty good. Bet that's the first time in a long time that anybody's sweet talked old Edna.

...

Word is that some boys snuck over to Manana last night and threw firecrackers in the shack while Kyriacos was sleeping. Probably Angus's sons because they're always up to something. And they love playing with fire! One time Randy saw them over by Christmas Cove launching fireworks at each other and had to tell Angus. Anyway, I told Randy to have a word with Angus about it because nobody wants to wake up to firecrackers at midnight.

September 1996

Yesterday I went to the sheep roast over on Manana and it was quite an event. Best party I've been to in a while and first time I've been to Manana since I don't know how long. Sure wouldn't want to live over there but it was nice to look back over the harbor and see home from the other side. I also enjoyed the row back home with Randy and seeing that big bonfire over there where it's usually so quiet and lonely-looking. I don't know how Kyriacos lives over there all alone, but he doesn't seem to mind. Last night he was the life of the party and must have made a dozen toasts just when Randy and I were there. Makes me wonder why we don't have more parties out here since they're so much fun.

...

Kyriacos stopped by the library the other day which was perfect timing because the author we had on the schedule for next month's reading at the library had to drop out and I asked Kyriacos if he'd read from his book. He said it was a real honor to be asked. He called his book a work-in-progress but said he could read ten or fifteen pages which sounded good to me. It always brings more people out when it's someone they know, and everybody out here knows Kyriacos by now. And on top of that it'll save the library some money since we don't have to pay for his ferry ride out here!

October 1996

Randy told me that the boys were talking today in the fish house about nicknames for Kyriacos. Randy says if you work on a boat you have to have a nickname. They thought of a bunch, but the ones I remember him telling me are K-Rock and Rockos. But would you believe it that in the end they decided on Bob. It sounds so boring to me but Randy says that's the point, that everybody can clearly see that Kyriacos isn't a Bob and that's what makes it funny. Like any nickname, maybe it'll stick, maybe it won't. As for me, I'll stick with Kyriacos.

...

Oh dear! About twenty people came to the reading last night and I think everyone left shaking their heads not knowing what to think. I would have never guessed by looking at him that he had that kind of stuff in his mind, but I guess you can never predict the creative types. When I talked with him last week he told me the book was about a lobster that wanted to learn how to swim like a fish. I figured that sounded like it would be good and clean but boy was I wrong. Those lobsters he wrote about—and especially the mussels!—talked dirtier than anyone I've ever met. Poor Ruth! She's come to every one of these readings but I don't know if she'll be such a big fan after last night. I suppose I'll have to make some house visits this week to clear things over so they don't think I planned it this way. If only I'd known!

November 1996

Kyriacos came to the library today and brought me two nice candles to thank me for asking him to do the reading last week. He said he was worried that maybe he had offended a few people and he apologized if he had caused me any trouble. He stayed for a long time and we had a real nice conversation. We talked about so many things. I haven't had a good conversation like that in a long time. He may have a strange imagination but he's curious and smart and a good talker. I showed Randy the candles and told him about our conversation and he teased me that Kyriacos was flirting with me but I told him yeah right.

...

Kyriacos had a friend come out to visit for a few days this month and they stopped by the library on their way out to the trails. Kyriacos said that he wanted to introduce the two of us because we both like mystery books. The friend said his favorite mystery writer is John Grisham who I like a lot but I told him my favorite is Angela Lansbury who writes all the <u>Murder, She Wrote</u> books. He was another good-looking guy with darker skin, bigger muscles than Kyriacos but shorter. They told me they'd been friends since kindergarten. I thought it was real nice of them to stop by. Anyhow, I heard that the friend spent a day on Buddy's boat but got pretty sick right from the start and spent the whole time leaning over the rails. That's one of the worst feelings in the world! That's why I only go out on calm days now, after you get that feeling once you never want it back again. That's one thing that Buddy really likes about Kyriacos, says he's never gotten sick on the boat.

December 1996

Kyriacos stopped by the library the other day to drop off a book and told me that he was going to visit his sister in Boston for a week. I asked him if he was going to spend Christmas with his family but he said he wanted to be back out here for Christmas. I don't know why anyone wouldn't want to be with their family for Christmas, but he must have a good reason. Lord knows families these days aren't what they used to be. Anyway, I didn't want him to be all alone on Manana so I invited him over to our place to eat Christmas dinner and I swear I thought he was going to cry. He came behind the desk and gave me a big hug and said he was looking forward to it.

...

Yesterday I got a letter from Kyriacos. I showed it to Randy and he asked if I was going to store it in a box with all my other love letters. Ha! Can you imagine? Here's the letter.[52]

> December 16, 1996
> Dear Evie,
> I'm writing from my sister's house in Brookline, Massachusetts, and I'm sorry to say that I won't be able to make it back up to Monhegan for Christmas. I was really looking forward to the dinner with you and your family, and I can't tell you how much your invitation meant to me. I'm happy to call you my friend. Maybe we can all do dinner together sometime in January when I return. I could even have all of you over for dinner on Manana if you don't mind eating dinner wrapped in blankets and sitting on the floor!
>
> My sister Selene has two kids and I've been taking them out to the playground every day this past week even though it's freezing cold outside. It seems even colder here than on Monhegan, which is strange since the island is thirteen miles off the coast. Though here everything is metal and concrete and the wind blows hard between the tall buildings and it just seems colder, even though it probably isn't.

---

[52]Evelyn regularly transcribes personal letters from friends and family members in her submissions.

I should tell you that I stopped working on my book (Scavengers) because I've felt stuck for the past few months. I really enjoyed it when I first started writing, but now it's just a pain and it makes me feel tired just to think about it. I've got another project in mind that I'll probably start working on when I get back to Monhegan (as long as Buddy doesn't work me too hard!).

I wish you, Randy, Cole, Curtis, and Soupie a very merry Christmas, and please know that I wish I could be there with you all.

Sincerely,
Kyriacos

January 1997

So Kyriacos came back a few day ago and brought a girl with him from what I hear. I didn't even know he'd come back until Randy saw smoke coming out of the chimney from over there one morning and teased me that my boyfriend must be back. I thought maybe Kyriacos would stop by the library with the girl but a few days went by and I didn't see them. I don't even think they crossed over to Monhegan that whole time. Too bad because I would have liked to meet her.

...

I heard this from Fred who's no gossip so I believe every word about what happened last night. He said that Olaf's daughter Anita took her dad's dinghy over to Manana in the middle of the night and started throwing a fit outside of Kyriacos' shack. Fred said he could hear it all loud and clear from his place by Fish Point. He said it sounded like Anita had gone mad for

Kyriacos and couldn't stand that girl being over there. Fred didn't hear what happened after the screaming stopped, but all he knows is that Anita made it back home and the other girl left on the ferry the next morning and that was that. I just can't believe Anita would get so jealous. I bet Olaf will ground her for the next ten years!

...

So this morning Marjorie told me that Kyriacos <u>did</u> come by the library when that girl was in town. She saw him knocking on the door one morning but it must have been after I got sick and had to stay at home on Tuesday. What a shame! I should have left a note for him down at the fish house but I don't want people to think I'm mad for Kyriacos like Anita was. Ha! They already joke enough that he's my boyfriend.

February 1997

I heard that Kyriacos and Chuckie got into a fight yesterday and Eddie had to break it up. He says that Kyriacos told Chuckie to stop shooting gulls from off the dock and Chuckie got upset. Chuckie's always had a bad temper. I remember he got real mad at Randy once on trap day when their boats bumped in the harbor. I think it's a shame when the boys shoot down gulls so I'm glad Kyriacos did what he did, but I don't know if he counted on throwing punches because of it. Only someone who didn't grow up here would pick a fight with Chuckie. Anyhow, Eddie said that they all went out and got drunk afterwards and cleared things up pretty good.

...

Boy is Randy going to be jealous! Kyriacos stopped by the library this morning and asked if he could start writing in the back room because it's too cold in his place over on Manana. I don't know how Ray lived over there for so long with such bad insulation, but this week was the real test. It was so cold and windy. Worse than I can remember. Even with the woodstove going full blast at the house we still have to wrap up in blankets most of the time. I can't imagine what it's like over there on Manana, but here in the library it's nice and warm and I think we'll have some good days working. It's always nice to have company.

March 1997

It's been real nice to have company these last few weeks. I sit at my desk by the entrance and Kyriacos works in the back room by the computer. He stays for a few hours each time and we spend half the time talking. I think he spends so much time with me mostly because he doesn't want to be working on that new project of his, but I don't mind. Randy says we're like an old married couple the way we go about our routine. I'm just glad to have someone to talk to since almost nobody ever comes in here in the winter.

April 1997

It was real hard to see Kyriacos leave yesterday. I knew he wasn't going to stay out here forever, but I didn't figure he'd leave so soon especially since he paid up the full year for Linda's boat. Of course he said he'd be back to visit next summer but you know how that goes. They all say that, and maybe they mean it, but then they get caught up in their lives on the mainland and never think about us again. There's so many young folks that come out here to work for the summers that usually I don't pay them any attention. Of course Randy keeps teasing me and said it's like we broke up or something, but he knows how lonely it can get in the library in the winter and I think he liked that someone was there to keep me company. It will sure feel empty there now that he's gone. He was good company and always had something interesting to say. Kept me on my toes! I think he meant it when he said that he'd come back and visit next summer. I don't know, I just have a feeling we'll see him out here again. Wouldn't that be nice.[53]

---

[53]According the Buddy Webster, Kyriacos never returned to Monhegan or Manana Islands after his departure in April 1997. His name does not appear in any of Evelyn's writings after this April 1997 submission.

Submission #12—Field Notes
Deer Isle—Penobscot Bay
Jack Charrette
4 September 1982

The coast of Maine has long attracted legions of recreational boaters and adventurers drawn to the rugged beauty of the landscape, the remote terrain, and the weather conditions that demand constant vigilance. The Hurricane Island Outward Bound,[54] established in 1964, is a testament to this adventurous spirit, as are the dozens of sailboats and sea kayaks that dot coastal Maine horizons during the summer. Individuals choose adventure at sea for many reasons—to test their skills or courage on water, to search for riches or answers that may lie below the surface, or to seek a calm, secluded harbor in which to relax and reflect.

This selection offers a deeply personal account of one man's solo kayak journey 113 miles up the Maine coast, from Portland to Friendship, seeking not so much adventure as an opportunity to spend time in nature, meditate on life, and reconnect with the landscape of his youth. The account, which includes self-selected excerpts from his detailed field notes, is as much a story of his journey through a physical landscape as it is through the landscape of his own emotional and psychological interior. He does not embark on the journey with any particular expectations or issues to resolve, but rather, as he writes, "with courage and humor and an open heart."

---

[54]Information about the Hurricane Island Outward Bound School can be found at https://www.hiobs.org

In 1982, when Jack Charrette took this seven-day journey, sea kayaking did not have the widespread popularity along the coast of Maine as it does today. This was before the time when the Maine Island Trail Association (MITA) developed an inter-connected trail of island campsites up the coast, or when sea kayak outfitters could be found in every small town along Route 1. When Jack took this trip he was part of a small, novel community. He saw only one other kayaker on his trip, whereas today he would likely have seen dozens before even getting out of Portland Harbor.

Much of Jack's biographical information is organically woven into the account of his kayak journey, therefore I will only specify that at the time of this trip he was living in Biddeford and working as a lab technician at the University of New England. Originally from Deer Isle, he left the island in 1960 and only returned once in 1971 for the funeral of his mother. Given that most Island Society members have a more direct and immediate connection to the islands, my first question for Jack, when I visited him at his Biddeford home in January 2016, was how his account ended up in the Island Files. He told me that he had never before heard of the Island Society and was both surprised to learn of its existence and that his writing had ended up in its possession. "After my trip," he said, "I felt a strong connection to the Maine coast and visited Deer Isle with Judy[55] in the summer of '83. By that time I'd turned my notes into a little booklet with drawings[56] and everything. It was

---

[55]Jack is referring to his wife, Judy Nelson-Charrette.

[56]Four of Jack's original sketches are part of this selection.

mostly for family and friends but I did give one copy to my Aunt Lynn. She was my only relative still on the island, and we were pretty close when I was growing up." The aunt he refers to is Lynn Marshall, a third-generation resident of Deer Isle with sixteen submissions in the Island Files.[57] Though it is probable that she submitted Jack's booklet, this is impossible to confirm given her death in 2011 and the fact that the submission was not accompanied by any introductory note.

"Field Notes" is the longest selection in this volume and is in fact the second longest submission in the entire Island Files.[58] Jack told me that the journal he kept during his trip ended up being quite long and that he selected only one memorable incident or recollection from each day to include in his booklet. He said that he wanted to draw out the gems of his trip and avoid having them get overshadowed by the more quotidian details of the journey. The result is a thoughtful account that is both a tribute to Jack's keen mind and courage as a kayaking pioneer, and also honors the journeys that we all take over challenging landscapes—physical, spiritual, psychological—at some point in our lives.

---

[57]None of her submissions appear in this volume, though one of her submissions will appear in *Volume III: Community.*

[58]The longest submission was submitted by Marsh Burns in the form of a draft short story entitled "The Last Hippie." He is also the author of "The South African," which appears earlier in this volume.

The Islands Within: Selected Field Notes from a Weeklong Ocean Kayaking Trip
by Jack Charrette

"I only went out for a walk and finally concluded to stay out till sundown, for going out, I found, was really going in."
—John Muir

In memory of Frank Wihbey,
Rainbow Walking

Note on Beginnings

Day 1: Encounter with a Harbor Seal (Portland's East End
     Beach to Jewell Island)

Day 2: A Sudden Storm (Jewell Island to Raspberry Island)

Day 3: Droppings (Raspberry Island to Perkins Island)

Day 4: The *Zendô* Stream (Perkins Island to Spectacle Island)

Day 5: Flotsam and Jetsam (Spectacle Island to Southport
     Island)

Day 6: Capsize (Southport Island to Thief Island)

Day 7: An Unexpected Swimmer (Thief Island to Friendship)

Coda

Note on Beginnings

This is the story of my seven-day journey by ocean kayak from Casco Bay to Muscongus Bay in the summer of 1982. Along the way I gathered impressions that you might expect from such a journey—seagull calls, salty air, scuttling crabs—though much of what I experienced was completely unpredictable, and internal, which is perhaps the reason why I chose to take this journey into Nature in the first place. This is also a story of how such a journey can be done, and why, and how it can change us. It can open new paths, both spiritual and psychological, that we never took the time to explore in our "normal" lives or that we never knew existed. This is my chronicle of paddling over 110 nautical miles and camping on six different islands in the Gulf of Maine. I present it here in short-form—as a series of meditations, observations, and wonderings extracted from the detailed journal I kept each day— in the hope that it might provide something of value to others contemplating a similar path.

What might distinguish this journey from others? Other kayakers have certainly paddled farther, better, and faster than I. Other writers, many of whom I admire, have done more dangerous, adventurous, and exciting things. For me this was a time to experience both pure solitude and physicality in nature, at length, in the middle of a busy life. I wanted to receive impressions directly and, with journal and drawing pad, record them as perceived. There was, finally, an opportunity to meditate, reflect, pray, and write, because there was time. Awakening, paddling, eating, and sleeping occurred, happily, according to natural rhythms of light and dark.

Many people have lost touch with what sustains them— simple, plentiful things, that nonetheless are felt to be distant or inaccessible. It is a sign of our times that this separation is now in the common awareness. And it explains the burgeoning surge of interest among the public in Nature, and on regaining a personal center. We have become vaguely aware that something may be off, that we have lost connection with a powerful energy, and by seeking a physical challenge in Nature we are at the same time accepting a trek on the uncharted landscape of our own psyche. This inner journey is often more demanding and consequential than the outer journey, though it can be difficult to articulate its impact to family and friends upon return. Yet we keep embarking on journeys, with all the struggles that they entail, ever seeking self-discovery and connection to something deeper and perhaps greater.

Even the planning of a journey has its risks. The journey is wherever life takes you. We plan some things. But mostly we plan to accept. We thrive at some things, fail at others. I had many chances to practice acceptance on my trip. I found endurance that I did not believe I had. I discovered that as a 53-year-old family man, new things can still begin. I thought a long time on the ocean about matters great and small: things undone or waiting to be done; friendship and its value; how one paces one's energy; and why one departs from the best and most sincere of intentions and resolutions under the pressure of the trivia of normal life.

How can I convey the transformation that took place from something as apparently simple as a long kayak trip in the ocean? It's hard to remember now: when did I first entertain the idea of such an excursion in the Gulf of Maine? The constellation of Maine islands—and island culture—have always held some fascination for me. Growing up as a boy on Deer Isle, attending the small school, and working delivery for Emmons Fuel Supply, I was impatient to get off the island, to plant my roots in the "civilized" mainland. Yet within the first few years of leaving the island I experienced a deep yearning to return to its shores. I never did return for long, however, not only because island friendships faded and family members passed away, but also because my roots gradually deepened on the mainland in form of home, career, and family. For over thirty years I was cheerfully consumed by the quotidian responsibilities of family and professional life, and though I lived only five miles from the ocean, the island existence of my childhood seemed a world away.

In the spring of 1975 my lab colleague Dale Skoog asked me if I wanted to go on a short ocean kayaking trip. I was at first intimidated: Dale was athletic, I was not. What happened if my kayak flipped? How long in the Gulf of Maine waters before I would succumb to hypothermia? Fortunately, Dale was a patient and generous teacher, and our first trip together was a very modest excursion around Richmond Island off the coast of Cape Elizabeth. This paddle rekindled my connection to the ocean and all that it evoked from my childhood. I took more trips with Dale, around Peaks Island and Chebeague Island in Casco Bay, out to Seguin Island off of Popham Beach. I eventually bought my own kayak and gear. My first solo trip was from East End Beach to Fort Gorges, a short paddle but one that made me anxious because of the heavy boat traffic in the channel crossing. All turned out fine, and I took many more short solo trips over the next few years, my wife Judy ever-supportive of this new endeavor.

I took my first overnight paddling trip to Jewell Island in Casco Bay in August 1978. I was amazed at the preparation that had to go into planning and packing for only one night away from home, yet the freedom of arriving on the island as an independent, self-reliant creature was exhilarating. Perhaps subconsciously, this is when the idea of an extended overnight journey by kayak up the Maine coast first took seed in my mind.

But I do remember an evening conversation in the summer, perhaps in July, when Judy and I were sitting at the picnic table—one of the rare times when the kids were otherwise occupied, and we had extended time together alone. Perhaps I was looking over nautical charts or glancing at an article about a plan to establish a coastal water trail that would connect over a hundred wild Maine islands. I probably came to some point in the conversation where I joked that the idea of paddling the entire Maine coast, over 375 miles, from Kittery to Lubec, was out of the question for me, at least at this point in my lifetime. And in fact, I really felt no deep desire to do so, then. With three teenagers at that point, I had plenty of adventure right at home. I could dream of someday embarking on a paddle from Portland to my old stomping grounds on Deer Isle —a homecoming of sorts—but that day lay in the distant future, perhaps when the kids were off to college. I wondered, though, if I would be healthy enough at that point in my life. Would I be too cautious in my older age to take off on a solo adventure? Would I have lost the will? Then Judy, perhaps sensing my anxieties, suggested that I plan a one-week trip for the following summer.

The idea took hold very seriously that evening. For the next few days I experienced a variety of feelings about the trip. One was a very understandable disquiet, a little bit of healthy fear. But there was another feeling in the background, harder to put my finger on. I eventually came to describe it as "renunciation." The purpose of this journey, after all, was to put aside the ordinary patterns and concerns, and to enjoy an immersion in Self and Nature the best that I could.

The renunciation feeling persisted for a couple of days. It was like a shock: how could I do this to myself, a trip of self-discipline, hardship, and a certain degree of austerity? I put away the idea of the trip without rejecting it, but also without telling anyone else. However, I did begin browsing the outdoor catalogues for a suitable cookstove.

Around Christmas I began to take up the idea again. My son Paul had just returned from a semester studying in China and was brimming with adventurous energy. We drank a beer together late at night at the kitchen table, his first beer in my presence, and he pushed me to take my own adventure. Despite what he expected to be a busy summertime schedule with a full-time landscaping job and baseball practice, Paul told me that if I did it next summer he would handle the transportation logistics and perhaps even join me for a night on one

of the islands. It was perhaps this gesture—or universal sign!
—that I needed, and I told Paul that I would take the trip.

Trepidation and self-doubt were there for me as I began
planning out the details. But also there was anticipation and
mystery. I had read stories of other long-distance ocean
kayakers who had written about getting "in the zone" and having "mystical, quasi-spiritual" experiences on their solo journeys. I had some idea of what they were talking about based
on my short trips, but I was curious to dive more deeply into
my own experience.

In late April, I had some additional inspiration. Dale invited me to a lecture and slide show by Nigel Foster, who had cir-
cumnavigated Iceland the previous year with his partner Geoff
Hunter. He showed striking images of raw Nature from the
perspective of a kayak, offered technical commentary, and
read excerpts from his book *Raging Rivers, Stormy Seas*. Nigel
additionally read excerpts from his personal journal at appropriate points and shared his doubts, triumphs, insights, and
appreciations. I identified strongly with his desire to embark
on the journey: the wish for solitude and silence, the appreciation of Nature, and the call to a personal challenge that must
be answered.

Again I realized that I must prepare mentally for the
inevitable: rain, discouragement, equipment failures and losses, unknown interactions with others, even minor injuries and
the question of whether to go on. Above all, however, I knew
that I must be well-prepared in terms of itinerary, equipment,
and self-rescue techniques. Though I knew that even "the best
laid plans" can fall apart, I did not want to find myself on a
long crossing without a float bag or a spare paddle. Nor did I
want to risk arriving at a beach only to find that I had forgot-
ten the can opener for my tuna lunch! In a true team effort,
my family helped me immensely with all of these details. Judy
and I went to L. L. Bean's outlet store in Freeport and rounded
out my supplies with some great bargains: a deck compass, a
paddle leash, a light-weight sleeping pad, and a used tent (for

$21), in excellent condition, that still smelled faintly of a man's cologne and had a few pine needles in it. Paul reviewed the charts with me and helped me map out an itinerary that avoided long open crossings and kept in mind my rather leisurely (some would say turtle-like) pace on the water. We confirmed the take-out location (Jameson Point docks in Friendship) and identified islands that were within reasonable distance from each other where I could camp each night. And my daughters, Stephanie and Angie, teamed up to purchase me a subscription to *Sea Kayaker* magazine for my birthday. I relished these magazines, and now that I was an official subscriber I somehow felt like I had crossed an important symbolic threshold.

In June I went on several long paddles in Casco Bay with a fully packed and outfitted kayak to "test the waters." At first the extra weight was unsettling and I thought I was going to capsize when a series of small waves struck me broadside. However, I gradually became accustomed to the full load and found it added stability in the swells. My main concern remained upper body strength and stamina. Would I have the endurance to paddle approximately fifteen miles a day for seven days? Would I have the strength at the end of a long day to drag my loaded kayak up a rocky beach out of the tidal zone? I continued taking these short trips throughout June, but still I knew that no training run could truly prepare me for the real thing. As I came to July, the anxiety built.

Now that I was ready in terms of logistics and equipment, there was the final matter of what I would carry with me in my heart and head. For fun, I decided to bring an old favorite, *The Lord of the Rings*, which seemed an appropriate book to bring on a journey. Knowing my eclectic reading habits, my family surprised me several days before the trip by presenting me with a waterproof binder filled with photocopied readings they thought might enrich my journey: "The Open Road" by Walt Whitman, "The Ledge" by Lawrence Sargent Hall, "The Clear Blue Lobster-Water Country" by Leo Connellan, and the mid-coast section of Fannie Hardy Eckstorm's classic *Indian Place*

Names of the Penobscot Valley and the Maine Coast. This gift filled me with such joy, and I later teased Judy that maybe I would have to cancel the trip in order to finish all of my reading.

A friend once asked me, perhaps only half-joking, whether my proposed trip was part of a mid-life crisis. I told him that it was just a short mid-life journey *into* Nature, not *away from* anything. In fact, preparing for the journey had actually gotten me closer to my family and more content at work. From the beginning, I hoped merely to respond in a tempered fashion to this inner call to challenge myself and immerse myself in the natural world. I looked forward to the cadence of paddling, the freedom from the daily cares, and the blessings of fresh air, sunlight, and tidal rhythms. I wondered, from time to time, about the nature of some of the feelings that I had while on the ocean: wordless, fleeting snapshots of emotion that I felt powerfully in a particular moment. For example, when I had paddled previously in a narrow channel between two bald granite isles, a beam of sunlight pouring out from behind an ominous-looking cumulonimbus, there had been a feeling of *dearness, intimacy, comfort, strength.* Another example was my unconscious reaction to looking up and seeing that my movements were being watched by three Great Blue Herons by the shores of Mackworth Island. There was the feeling, not articulated, but rather felt: *we are all, simultaneously, in intimacy with the Earth.*

My final weeks before the trip were spent mostly in the business of final preparations, much of which was fun, some of which was tedious or gave me slight pangs of guilt. I would miss, for example, the final performance of Angie's summer choral camp, I wouldn't be able to attend two of Paul's baseball playoff games, and I was leaving Judy with all the housework for a full week. I expressed my regret to each of them and they told me not to be silly. Judy pointed out that I was having last-minute jitters about the trip, and said that I wasn't getting out of it that easily!

Several nights before my scheduled departure I was leafing through a pile of old *National Geographic* magazines that had accumulated in our basement and came across a photo-journalistic piece that had struck me as remarkable when I had read it several years earlier. In the piece, a well-known Nature photographer, Jim Brandenburg, challenges himself to go into the north woods of Minnesota for 90 days, between the autumnal equinox and the winter solstice, and take only one photograph a day. As someone accustomed to shooting hundreds of pictures a day, this was a test of self-discipline, of truly capturing the decisive moment and committing to one image above all others. I found this challenge of self-restraint fascinating, and I wondered how I could contrive a similar test for myself on this journey. Only later that night, as I was falling asleep, did it occur to me that this chronicle of my journey would be a suitable place to exhibit such restraint. So at the last minute my idea for this chronicle took a different direction than I had been planning: rather than providing a detailed account of the trip with descriptions of weather patterns and campsites and wildlife sightings, it would instead focus only on the experiences, sensations, feelings, or impressions that were most resonant from each day. I would make an effort to focus on just one, in the spirit of Mr. Brandenburg, though I wasn't interested in being too strict. I didn't know what this would look like, or whether it would be difficult or worthwhile, but it felt right when I settled on it.

I brought with me to the ocean, then, thoughts of the family, what I felt was the requisite gear, and also some hints about the deeper feelings I might experience on the journey. I hoped to find inner resources beyond what I knew I had, and to approach the journey with courage and humor and an open heart. Yet no matter what expectations I had, or preparations I had made, I still resolved to let this journey take its own shape and tell its own story.

Day 1: Encounter with a Harbor Seal

There is a small, crescent-shaped beach on Jewell Island that can be accessed via a narrow path from the campsite. It is protected by a large rock formation that juts out of the water about fifty yards offshore, so its waters are calm and there are no waves. An assortment of driftwood and plastic bottles and seaweed clumps gently wash back and forth on the shoreline, and the water is a frothy dark-blue. I know that it will be very cold, but I am sweaty after a day of paddling and I decide to swim.

I leave my clothes in a pile on the beach and wade cautiously over the uneven rocks into deeper water. The sun is hot on my bare skin and there is a light onshore breeze that has the strong smell of fish. I shiver involuntarily when my knees reach the water, though I persevere and go deeper. Several yards further and I plunge in, not diving forward for fear of unknown rocks below the surface, but rather curling myself into an underwater ball and sinking into the water. I give myself a quick sub-aquatic scrub and spring back to the surface. I repeat this several more times and then stand still in the water, bellybutton-deep, looking out over the Atlantic Ocean. Two mergansers float nearby, seemingly oblivious to my presence. But I also see a harbor seal poking his mottled-grey head above the water about thirty yards away. We watch each other for a moment, then he disappears. I stand motionless, scanning the water's surface, and see him reappear seconds later, fifteen yards closer. Now I can clearly see his eyes —round, watery black holes that appear lifeless from a distance. I feel there is something haunting about his eyes, and again I shiver. I wonder how many seals are out there. Do seals usually come this close to shore? I suddenly feel unprotected and self-conscious, my body vulnerable beneath the surface. I edge my way back over the sharp rocks and onto the shore, eager for warmth and cleanliness, but also eager to get back to safety.

Drying off in the sun, I wonder why my first impulse was to feel threatened by the seal. Why did I not instead feel comfort at having a companion in the water? I know very well that seals are harmless and curious creatures, yet I still felt exposed. I dig my toes into the sandy beach and feel that I need to put my finger on what haunted me about this incident. I am reminded of the first time I heard a loon call, on Sabattus Pond, and how it was beautiful, but also how it quickly made my mind race toward danger. I eventually arrive at the idea that the source of my disquiet is "the unknown." When the seal gazed at me with his otherworldly puppy eyes my mind wondered what lay beneath the surface. This is perhaps an instinct, though I worry that it is also an impediment to connecting with Nature. How do I let down this instinctual guard in order to experience Nature in the most authentic way?

I smile as this thought passes through my mind and appreciate the irony of the scene: I stand naked on a beach in the wilderness asking myself how I can let down my guard even more. The black flies begin coming out as the sun lowers and I put my clothes back on. The swim has made me hungry and I walk back up to camp to begin preparing dinner, my interaction with the seal an indelible and poignant memory from the day.

Day 2: A Sudden Storm

It is a humid mid-afternoon and a crack of thunder echoes in the distance. Heavy, dark clouds drive in low and hard from the southwest and the winds begin shifting. A nervous, crackling energy fills the air and I know that I must get off the water soon. The closest land is Turnip Island—a small, rocky, bulb-shaped protrusion—and I drag my kayak up its gravelly beach as a light rain begins to fall. There is one house on Turnip (likely a vacation house and currently unoccupied), and I take refuge under the eaves of its wraparound veranda.

The storm begins in earnest shortly after I settle in, and I have a glorious view of the spectacle. A furious gust of wind whips over the water and is followed by a pounding haze of rain. The day becomes darker. I see one sailboat over by Haskell Island rocking back and forth precariously. Thunder and lightning move closer, their detonations over the ocean both startling and miraculous. The ocean churns with choppy whitecaps and I am glad to be safe and dry on land. I notice a flock of seagulls bobbing on the waves, seemingly unfazed by the inhospitable conditions, and I admire their resilience.

My nook on the veranda is cozy and keeps me mostly dry. I snack on peanut butter and crackers and feel a primeval thrill at being close to danger yet so secure. I consider how if I were at home I may have only given passing notice to such a storm, maybe even considered it an inconvenience, yet out here I feel as though I am experiencing something remarkable and almost divine. The storm's fury demands my full presence, and I feel a sense of triumph and accomplishment just for bearing witness to it.

The storm tails off, and I hear the thunder's rumblings as it moves up the coast. A cleansing stillness descends momentarily on the landscape. This afternoon I feel that I shared an hour of magical intensity with Nature—I experienced something very real and unmitigated, and I am full of appreciation. A soft, warm rain falls and I drag my kayak back to the water.

My campsite on Raspberry Island is at least two hours of steady paddling from here, and I am happy to be back on the water.

Day 3: Droppings

I awake very early and eat a bowl of granola and powdered milk on the rocks overlooking Small Point. The beginning of each day in the wilderness seems a blessing, and I feel a great sense of inner calm as the sun begins its steady rise from the east. While sitting there, in no particular rush to pack up camp and get a start on the day's paddle, I notice a remarkably large pile of animal droppings—large, light-brown pellets— underneath a nearby conifer tree. Raspberry is a very small island, about a quarter mile from shore, and it surprises me to think that a sizeable mammal might live here. I put down my bowl and walk over to the droppings. They are not fresh, and though I know very little about animal scat, I think the pellets are too large to be from a deer. I wonder what animal could have left this behind, and if that animal is still here.

I pick up a stick and poke at the pile. The droppings are consistent in color and thoroughly dried out. Each dropping is egg-shaped—though smaller than a chicken egg—and slightly pointed at one end. They look fibrous and earthy. My probing yields no clues and I consider the possibilities. Bear and moose seem unlikely, given the island's distance from the mainland. Coyote scat would be shaped more like that of a dog. For some reason owl comes to mind, but I quickly realize this is absurd given the size of the pile. What about a wild sheep? I know they used to inhabit many Maine islands,[59] and perhaps a small population—or even a lone sheep—still lives on Raspberry and does a good job of staying out of sight.

---

[59]The fascinating history of sheep on many Maine islands can be found in Philip Conkling's *Island in Time,* pages 88-92.

I rinse out my breakfast bowl in the tidal zone and continue contemplating the mystery droppings. It is still early, and I decide to explore the island in search of clues. My curiosity is piqued, and I feel playful and free as I launch into this jolly, low-stakes investigation. It takes me twenty minutes to walk the circumference of the island and I scan the ground for tracks or scat. I then walk across the island from several angles, up a small incline of boulders, through a dense stand of what I believe to be jack pines, hoping to rustle a sheep (though hopefully not a bear) from its hiding place. I enjoy the walk, and the sense of purpose that comes with such an excursion, but I find nothing to advance my case.

Knowing that I cannot linger all day on this mystery, yet not wanting to leave it behind entirely, I return to the droppings with my drawing pad. This is a case to be solved at a later date.

Day 4: The Zendô Stream

The campsite on Spectacle Island is a round clearing shaded by aspen trees and encircled that of a *zendô*, a Zen Buddhist monastery, where people may go when they by a lush, knee-high carpet of bracken fern. A small stream trickles nearby, barely audible, its banks lined with moss-covered stones and several rotting logs. Flat, oval-shaped rocks line the path from the beach to the clearing, and a large slab of granite juts out of the earth at an angle that make it seem more sculptural than natural. Unlike the other campsites I have visited so far on my journey, this one gives the impression that it has been deliberately designed and cultivated by someone who cares for this space and probably visits here often. The ambiance feels like wish to have a quiet place to meditate.

How glad I am to be at this campsite at the end of a long afternoon paddle against strong headwinds. I soak my feet in the stream's icy, bubbling waters and watch a water strider approach my calves, then quickly flit away as she presumably decides they will offer no sustenance. For several moments I close my eyes and listen to the flowing water. The surface is in a constant state of tumbling, splashing and foaming—full of energy and potential. I detect a richness in the flow and fall of the water, a series of subtle sounds that go beyond the soothing "white noise" that I heard upon first sitting down. What I hear now is also pleasant, but it isn't uniform—it is punctuated, rather, with little plocks and bumps and splash "events" that do not seem to repeat. This is chaotic activity and it leaves a strong impression on my mind. Maybe this is why people sometimes think they hear voices and perhaps other mystical sounds in water. People are always seeing the familiar in the chaotic. It must be our nature to pick out patterns to discern meaning that might pertain to our lives and fortunes.

I light up my cookstove later that evening and a final story occurs to me on the theme of water: In *The Lord of the Rings*, after the Forest Elves welcome Frodo and his companions, Frodo tells them he heard a voice in the waters that formed the boundary of their land. "Ah yes," they say. "You are hearing the voice of Nimrodel, after whom the stream is named. It is an ancient story."

Day 5: Flotsam and Jetsam

Lower Mark Island is a potato-shaped granite mound that sits in the outer mouth of the Sheepscot River. I stop there for a bathroom break in the early afternoon and drag my boat up the pebbly shore through a cluttered and entangled band of seaweed-strewn flotsam (or is it jetsam?) that sits just above the high-tide line. It is a messy scene, with large flies hovering over mangled lobster traps, plastic bottles, knots of rope, bleached driftwood, and car tires. It is a stark reminder that wilderness cannot escape the imprints of humanity.

I stand on a sand dune looking down at the immense clumps of debris and find them both depressing and fascinating. These objects have all found their way to this marine junkyard because of the flow of tides and currents, not because of some greater human plan. Each of these bleached and salt-encrusted objects has taken on its own unplanned journey to arrive here, and I wonder about their stories. Why is there a car bumper in the pile? How did the plastic stool end up here? Who does that yellow and black buoy belong to? I also wonder what will become of these objects. Will they be swept back to sea by the next storm? Will they remain on this beach and decompose gradually, as one large, interconnected mass?

I eat from my box of raisins and walk down to the pile for closer inspection. I have the feeling, like all treasure hunters, that there must be some hidden gem amongst all of this garbage, some remarkable object that was swept off the deck of a sailboat, perhaps, by a sudden gale. I hunt through the various heaped entanglements like I am at a rummage sale hoping to find a bargain. I am surprised by my own eagerness as a junkyard shopper. Yet, as I make my way to the far end of the beach, I observe that there is little diversity among the objects and scarce chance that anything of real interest could end up here.

I glance up at the sun and am suddenly disappointed that I have spent so much time exploring these piles. Why was I so drawn to them? What was I hoping to find? Where did this materialist, consumer urge come from within me? I consider these questions as I paddle away, well-rested but without any "treasure," my kayak leaving behind no lasting impression of my visit to the island, only a thin, fading line of wake.

Day 6: Capsize

Wisps of mid-morning fog hover over the water and I hug close to the shore around Pemaquid Point. The sun looks like a hazy yellow globe ready to burst through the translucent layer of low clouds, and I know the day will soon become hot. A fishing boat passes nearby, followed by a flock of cawing seagulls. The constellation of lobster buoys in Muscongus Bay all lean seaward in the outgoing tide. I rest my paddle on the cockpit and look back over my left shoulder at the Pemaquid Point Lighthouse rising sturdily above the mist – a majestic scene, captured in a golden glow. I turn my entire body to get a better view. It is a beginner's error, and I capsize immediately and mercilessly into the swift-moving open waters off Lighthouse Cove.

For my first capsize, I had vaguely anticipated having a slow-motion descent into the water, one of those timeless moments where I would see my life flash before my eyes. But this is instant and involves no thinking, no reflection. I am simply underwater upside-down and have to react. I push myself out of the boat and gasp to the surface, in near-disbelief of my situation, more surprised than cold, not knowing exactly what to do next. Land is so close but made inaccessible by the waves pounding against the craggy shoreline. The fishing boat is long gone and I see no other boats on the horizon. I am alone, and I must self-rescue.

Once I accept my situation and acknowledge what must be done, I become methodical. The winter practice sessions at the Biddeford YMCA swimming pool have paid off. As I gather the necessary self-rescue equipment from my deck bungees, I feel composed and unhurried. It occurs to me that I am experiencing a sort of rite of passage, an event that marks an important stage in my life as a kayaker. To not experience this would be to always live with a lurking self-doubt: *what if* that happened to me? I have dreaded this very moment since I began kayaking four years ago and have done much to avoid it. Now that it is here, however, I see that my dread was simply grounded in the unknown.

Back in the boat, I stop a few hundred yards down the shore at Pumpkin Cove to regroup. I am wet, cold, and worried about my gear, but I am also exhilarated. I have conquered one of my fears. I have been baptized by the waters of the Gulf of Maine. I lay out my soaked gear on the beach and feel a deep sense of relief. Is this not why one takes such journeys?

Day 7: An Unexpected Swimmer

I feel light-hearted on this final morning of my journey and I play a kayak game that involves weaving between the innumerable lobster buoys of Muscongus Bay. This is a good way of practicing my sweep stroke and, like a slalom racer, I tack right and left between a tight line of buoys, aiming toward Hog

Island. I am exhausted after twenty or so buoys and allow myself to glide silently on the water, appreciating the distinct color patterns of each buoy and wondering about the stories or symbols behind these colors.

Scanning the waterline, I see what I at first believe to be an unusually large harbor seal several hundred yards in the distance. It moves through the water at a steady pace, with a slight up-and-down bob, and I quickly recognize that it is much too large, and swimming too awkwardly, to be a seal. I paddle toward the creature, my curiosity drowning out any sense of fear, and am astonished to realize that it is a moose.

It is a magical scene: a large woodland mammal swimming somewhat gracefully in the ocean at least a quarter mile from the closest land. Was this possible? I had never heard of this happening before. Where was the moose going? What was it searching for out at sea? I give the moose a wide berth as it passes by, not knowing its potential in the water and not wanting to agitate it. Many questions come to mind as I watch the moose make its way through the multi-colored buoys out into the deeper waters of Muscongus Bay, and I suddenly wish I had brought a camera on the journey.

I trail in the moose's wake for a half hour at a respectful distance, hoping to better understand her intentions or destination. Yet she seems to be headed nowhere in particular, already having passed Cow Island and not directed toward any of the larger islands in the bay. This seems an existential moment for the moose: to continue swimming is to die. I can think of no other possibility, and I wonder if I should intervene. But what could I do? There is an unknowable force driving the moose onward through the water, and who am I to intervene with the inscrutable ways of the natural world? I wish the moose well in its journey and turn my bow back in the direction of the mainland.

Coda

Six months have now passed since I pulled into Friendship Harbor. It has been a long and valuable period of recollection and examination. I can't say I experienced any dramatic life changes after I returned from my journey. No one, perhaps, should expect so much from so modest a journey. But I did find afterward that I had more energy for the tasks of my profession. I found just a little bit more self-encouragement to start projects involving leadership, public speaking, writing, and service. And I even became more helpful to my family with their needs.

Although I traveled light, there were a few things I brought back that I would count as "souvenirs." I have a beard now. I did not shave while on the water. When I returned I decided to keep it for a while. Maybe deep down I felt it was a visible sign to myself and to other people of "after the Journey." In December, I finally found the will to quit my evening ritual of drinking a beer or two, having given this abstention a successful test during the paddle. I also felt physically stronger after the journey, and though strange muscles in my upper back were sore for nearly two weeks after my return, I experienced that soreness wistfully, as a sentimental reminder of my time at sea, instead of as an annoyance.

Perhaps my greatest growth on this journey occurred in my relationship with the Gulf of Maine. I reconnected with this landscape and its creatures in a powerful and profound way. It led me to moments of wonderment, surprise, difficulty, and self-discovery. It revealed deeper layers of itself with each passing day. I inhaled its fresh salt air, paddled through its lobster-rich waters, and found a great sense of permanence in its granite islands. I believe it is safe to say that this landscape still has much to teach me, and that my journey through the Gulf of Maine has only just begun.[60]

---

[60]Jack told me that he has taken three extended overnight kayak trips in the Gulf of Maine since his 1982 journey. In 1993, he kayaked the coast of Baja California for three days with his friend and colleague Dale Skoog.

Postscript

Everything is held together with stories.
—Barry Lopez

In final analysis, what are we to make of the Island Society?

On the one hand, I am inclined to set aside attempts at interpretation and to simply accept the unknown. This is the part of me that yearns to leave more to the imagination, to live in a world with a deeper appreciation for the magic and the wonder that are imbedded deep in the very construct of the Island Society. I would argue, after all, that there is a particular sense of beauty, elegance, and confidence in allowing certain mysteries to exist, in leaving a spot or two of uncharted territory on the map.

On the other hand, the desire to seek truth and meaning is central to human nature. To leave stones unturned and riddles unsolved is often an embarrassment to our ever-theorizing, modern minds. However romantic the notion may be of simply accepting the unknown, it is difficult, perhaps unrealistic, not to inquire further when so many essential questions remain.

Whichever of these paths a reader decides to take—that of romantic acceptance or that of persistent inquiry—my hope is that these selections instill in all readers an appreciation not only for the culture of island communities and the natural environment of coastal Maine, but also for the richly diverse and unique voices of individuals who voluntarily contributed their writings to this peculiar and grand idea. However implausible the Island Society may sound as an organization, and despite the myriad questions that its underground existence leaves behind, the fact remains that it served a vital role for its far-reaching membership base. After all, why did so many people from such a broad demographic choose to send off their writing to an unknown destination for over three generations? What inspired their faith in this process? What made them willing to show such vulnerability? In short, what compelled these people?

A comprehensive review of the remaining Island Files archive, and more specifically of the twelve selections in this volume, suggests that each submission could be associated with at least one of three main motivating factors. For some, the Island Society offered an opportunity for *personal reflection*. Consider Jack Charrette's poetic musings from his kayak journey along the Maine coast, Frank Hamilton's emotionally raw apologia to his sons, and Edith Gilbert's heartbreaking homage to the Mercer family. In all of these cases, the reader is invited deep inside the authors' hearts and minds as they reflect on profound memories and experiences.

For others, the process of writing their submissions served as an opportunity to *reflect on personal disappointment or community tragedy*. In many of these submissions, writing seems to be a therapeutic act, an occasion to process what has happened through the written word. Consider Dean Sullivan's chain-smoking regret about arriving too late for the bikini contest, Arnetta Sidwell's heartfelt concern for others in the wake of the Baptiste kayak tragedy, and Natasha Pixley-Miller's lyrical account of the sorrowful and softening beekeeper. Indeed, some variation of tragedy or disappointment seems to lie at the heart of many of these selections, from the brutal revenge in "The South African" to the loss of companionship in "Kyriacos" to the haunting sense of loneliness in the melodies of "Manana." Yet regardless of the magnitude of the disappointment or tragedy recounted these stories, each author shares an emotionally poignant episode from their own life, and often from the life of their tight-knit island community as well.

Still for others, the act of sending in submissions served as an opportunity to *fulfill one's institutional duty*. Generally straight-forward, light-hearted, and employing plain, down-to-earth language, the majority of the Island Files archives is comprised of this category of submissions. Here we have members simply fulfilling their duty to the Island Society. Constance Moody, for example, wrote 96 submissions mostly about the weather and what she saw from her kitchen window. Bunny Mann wrote 57 submissions mainly describing routine community affairs and fishing conditions. And over the years, countless other members wrote such "business-as-usual" submissions that would likely be of little interest to those outside of their community, yet when read collectively, these are the submissions that help create a compellingly realistic and authentic socio-cultural portrait of the Gulf of Maine's island communities.

Underlying each of these motivating factors is a deep sense of purpose, whether it be the opportunity to reflect, to ease one's pain, to give a sense of meaning to the mundane, to gain satisfaction at fulfilling one's duty, to feel a sense of belonging in one's community, and perhaps to seek connection to the outside world. As readers will see in the forthcoming volumes of the *Island Files*, *Conflict* and *Community*, one of these overarching motivations is clearly evident in each selection. Members wrote, and they wrote with intention. That intention, it could be argued, served a higher purpose that, as non-members, we will perhaps never fully understand.

***

During my third and final meeting with Linwood Judd, on the afternoon of September 21, 2012, we sat in lawn chairs on his back porch drinking Nescafé and looking out over the rough, dark-green waters of Frenchman's Bay. Linwood was by nature a pragmatic man, well-suited to the hardships and deprivations of island life, and disinclined to question conventional wisdom or to speculate about matters that were beyond his immediate understanding. Yet on this afternoon, perhaps because I would soon be departing with the last four crates of Island Files submissions and thereby relieving him definitively of the role of Master Wickie, he became unguarded for a moment and shared with me an enigmatic musing about the founding of the Island Society. "I imagine it started," he said, "to hold us all together. That was the higher purpose, I think, to keep us awake, and to hold us all together."

I have given these lines a great deal of consideration over

the past five years and have come to believe that Linwood hit on something, in that brief moment of reflection, that lies at the very heart of the Island Society's *raison d'être*. I now see the archive of submissions—this remarkable collection of diverse and uncensored stories—as a secondary function of the Island Society. These stories are merely the byproduct of members' profound sense of belonging and commitment to a place, a region, and a way of life that is buried deep inside their hearts. The call to "maintain written documentation of particular occurrences," as stated in the 1916 Island Society memorandum, is essentially a call to remain awake to, and present in, one's surroundings, and to not forget that one is an integral part of something much larger and deeply interconnected. By tapping into this psychology of awareness and belonging, the Island Society helped create a mighty yet discreet community of proud islanders who, against many odds, stuck together and oftentimes thrived for over three generations in a remote, spirited, and magnificently resilient corner of the world.

Acknowledgements

I am greatly indebted to Adèle Saint Pierre for her assistance with *The Island Files.* Without her this book would not exist. It's as simple as that. As always, I am humbled by her creativity, humanity, editorial brilliance, and fierce work ethic.

I am also grateful to the following individuals for their support in reading and offering feedback on *The Island Files*: John Wihbey, Ian Garthwait, Eugene May, Don Gibson, Zac Pelleriti, and of course Nancy, Scott, and Zack. A wise, generous, and oftentimes rowdy bunch.

I thank Qiannong Wu for providing the drawings in "Field Notes."

The idea for *The Island Files* came to me in 2017 when I spent the summer in Portland, Maine, working for my brother's sea kayak company, Portland Paddle. I thank the incredible crew at Portland Paddle for their kindness and patience with me as I sharpened my kayak guiding skills in Casco Bay.